AF432204

CONTENTS

DREAM CATCHER

Jamal woke up with a start. Sweating profusely and with his pulse racing, he flung his covers off to the side and leapt out of bed. Wiping his forehead with the back of his hand, he made his way to the bathroom to splash some cold water on his face.

After toweling himself dry, he peered at his face in the mirror and was not happy with the image he saw staring back at him. The lack of sleep was starting to show in his visage. Not being able to sleep for more than a few hours at a time for weeks on end will do that to a person.

A suddenly loud scratching sound coming from behind snapped him out of his thoughts as he spun around to catch the source. Seeing nothing, Jamal began to gingerly walk to the doorway of the bathroom. Slowly peering out into the hallway, he looked left and then right.

He fumbled for the light switch and flicked it on. Nothing. All was quiet. He walked back to his bedroom and turned on the light, but everything was as he left it. Glancing at the clock on his nightstand he saw that it was only three in the morning.

Shaking his head, he was sure he heard something but maybe the lack of sleep was starting to make him go a little loopy. That's when the sound returned, only louder this time and it was followed by a low animalistic growl.

The hairs on the back of his neck stood at attention as he caught a glimpse of something in the floor-length mirror. Jamal's breath caught in his throat as he spun around for the second time. The creature, covered in charcoal-grey fur towered over him.

It grabbed Jamal with massive taloned hands and lifted him up off his feet while opening its' huge mouth wide, revealing large spike-like teeth. As it pulled him closer to its' now drooling lips, Jamal let out an ear-piercing scream.

This time he woke up for real in bed sweating and screaming, startling his boyfriend, Tank. "Hey," Tank said after grabbing Jamal. "You're okay. You were having another nightmare. Was it the same one?"

"Yes and no," Jamal said as he sat upright. "This was more real. That thing always kept its' distance. It never, I mean this thing grabbed me and was going to fucking eat me!"

"Hon, it was just a nightmare. It isn't real."

It was then that Jamal realized he had something in his hand. He unclenched his fist and gasped.

"What?" Tank asked. "What is it?"

Jamal turned the nightstand lamp on and held up his open hand for Tank to see. "If it's not real, then what the hell is this?"

Tank stared in disbelief at the clump of dark fur in his partner's hand. "What the f...?"

The next morning, Jamal was seated in the waiting area of Webster's Sleep Research Institute, in Bala Cynwyd, Pennsylvania. The large, three-story building sits just off City Line Avenue. Jamal was exhausted and smiled politely as Tank arrived with a big cup of black coffee.

"Thanks hon," he said. "I really need this. Are you okay? You look like you're ready to jump out of your skin!"

"Babe, it's you I'm worried about. I just wish I had an explanation for that handful of fur! That's what's freaking me out more than anything!"

"Well, I must admit that it's got me a little unhinged too! Does this mean that thing in my nightmares is real?"

"That's what we're here to discover." Startled, Jamal and Tank jumped. "I'm so sorry about that. I didn't mean to startle you. I'm Dr. Gary Perez. I'll be working with Jamal Robinson."

Jamal stood up and said, "That's me and this is my boyfriend, Tank."

The doctor shook their hands and said, "It's nice to meet you both. Please, follow me and we can talk in my office."

Once they reached the doctor's office, he opened the door and gestured for them to take a seat in front of his desk. He closed the door and then took a seat in his chair.

Before he could speak again, Jamal said, "Thank you for squeezing me in with such short notice. We are both starting to freak out and I honestly don't know what I would've done if I couldn't be seen by someone today."

Dr. Perez placed a file on the desk in front of him and said, "It wasn't a problem at all. Your case is why we are here, to get to the root cause of your nightmares. In fact, we are getting ready to launch an experimental sleep study. We needed just one more volunteer and I happen to think that you'd be an excellent candidate."

"Really?" Tank asked. "What kind of sleep study?"

Dr. Perez smiled and said, "I'll circle back to that and explain in a minute, but first, I have the results back from the clump of fur that you brought in. The results are conclusive. The hair or fur is canine in nature. Since dogs and wolves share ninety-eight-point eight percent of their DNA, we are unable to differentiate any further."

Jamal and Tank appeared worried and reached out to hold each other's hand.

Dr. Perez cleared his throat and continued, "Now I have the information from the intake here in your file, but I'd like to hear it directly from you, how you came to acquire this sample."

Jamal leaned back, crossed his legs, took a deep breath, and said, "You're going to think I'm crazy but going back three or four weeks now, I've been having trouble sleeping. I have this recurring nightmare where I'm being stalked by…"

Dr. Perez leaned forward and said, "It's okay, Jamal. I promise I'm not here to judge you. I don't think you're crazy. Please, continue."

"It's a freaking werewolf! I was never sure before because I would never actually see it, but last night… It grabbed me and pulled me towards its open mouth. Somehow, I must have pulled it's fur out of the dream when I woke up, but how is that possible?"

"Well, that's what we're here to find out, which leads me into explaining the sleep study. I've always believed that our dreams, or even nightmares, are trying to tell us something. Relay messages to us, so-to-speak."

Dr. Perez could see that he'd already lost Jamal and Tank. He closed Jamal's file, stood up and said, "Follow me. It may be easier to just show you what I mean." Jamal and Tank silently nodded yes and got up to follow the doctor out of the office, down the hall and to some elevator banks.

They entered a car once one arrived and watched the doctor scan his badge underneath the elevator buttons. Once a green light came on, the doctor pushed the button for the basement. The three of them remained silent during the descent and upon reaching their destination, Tank and Jamal followed Dr. Perez to another office.

This one was made entirely of glass and was set up as a sort of observation room. Two staffers, dressed all in white, were busy messing with consoles and paperwork, On the other side of the room was another with a bunch of equipment, hospital beds and there were three people pacing around in the area wearing white hospital gowns.

Dr. Perez entered first and said, "Dr. Garcia, Dr. Miller, I'd like to introduce you to Jamal and Tank. Jamal, if he is willing, may be the fourth candidate that we've been looking for to include in our study."

Dr. Miller was the first to speak as he shook their hands. He said, "Excellent! We'd be happy to have you, Jamal. This is an exciting opportunity for all concerned!"

Dr. Perez then turned to Dr. Garcia and said, "Jeffrey, I made a feeble attempt trying to explain to these two what it is that we're trying to do here. Would you mind...?"

Dr. Garcia shook Jamal and Tank's hands before saying, "Yes, of course. I'd be happy to. We call this the dream catcher program. See the monitors above our heads?"

Jamal and Tank looked above, then nodded yes, so Dr. Garcia then gestured to the adjacent room where the other subjects, or patients were. He then continued, "For our sleep study, we attach electrodes to our subjects, which allows their dreams to be projected onto the screens, or monitors. That's an oversimplification, but we also administer a drug that allow the test subjects to enter to and interact in each other's dreams as well. Everything is projected live as it's happening and recorded to be reviewed as we see fit, to catch something we might have missed upon initial viewing. As you know, dreams do not always make sense to us, so this procedure will allow us to delve a little deeper."

Jamal took a deep breath and exhaled as he ran his hand over his head. He then said, "Okay. I'm following you but this all seems a little far-fetched to me. Walking into another person's dreams and experiencing what they are experiencing? I'm sure Dr. Perez filled you in on my case. Aren't you at all concerned that this could be dangerous for everyone involved?" The doctors all exchanged knowing smiles amongst themselves. For some reason, this irritated Jamal.

Dr. Perez was the first to pick up on that and decided to immediately address it. "Look, Jamal, we appreciate your hesitance and we do take it seriously, but to Dr. Garcia's point, dreams shouldn't always be taken literally. It's often a metaphor for something else. A werewolf, for instance is symbolic of fear or repressed anger."

"Okay," Jamal said, "Then how do you account for the fur?"

"Well, you got me there! But if you consent to the dream analysis, excuse me, dream catcher program, we can find out the answers together."

Jamal looked at Tank who shrugged and nodded his head yes, indicating that Jamal should go for it. He returned his attention to Dr. Perez and said, "Okay, fine. I'll do the program under one condition."

"What's that?" Dr. Miller asked.

Jamal pointed to the adjacent room and said, "That we disclose to those poor souls in there what they may be in for."

Smiling, Dr. Garcia handed Jamal a clipboard and hospital gown and said, "Consider it done! You can get changed behind that screen over there. There's a table with a plastic bag that you can put your personal effects in. Once you've changed, we'll introduce you to your new dream mates."

Jamal accepted the items and asked, "Can Tank stay and observe?"

"Absolutely!" Dr. Perez said.

Jamal gave Tank a quick kiss and said, "I love you! Thank you for being here."

Tank smiled and said, "Of course! I love you too!"

Once Jamal went behind the screen to get changed, Tank asked, "Is there a bathroom I can use before things get underway here?"

"There is," Dr. Perez said as he guided Tank through the door, "Go down this hallway to the left and the men's room is on the right."

"Thank you, doctor."

"No problem at all."

Jamal came from behind the screen and said, "Okay, I'm ready."

"Excellent!" Dr. Garcia said. "Okay, follow me."

Jamal followed the doctor into the adjacent room where the current occupants stopped pacing and turned in unison at the sound of Dr. Garcia's voice. "Good morning, everyone! I'd like you to meet the final member of our group, Jamal Robinson. Please introduce yourselves and the recurring dream that brings you in today."

The first person to step up seemed shy and timid. She had long and straight waist-length brown hair and green eyes that looked haunted. Jamal recognized the look. She obviously was having trouble sleeping as well. "Hi," she said. "My name is Nadia. In my dreams I'm a skilled fighter and warrior."

Jamal nodded and shook her hand. The next person that stepped up was a blonde male in desperate need of a haircut with hazel eyes. He also appeared to be sleep deprived. He extended his hand and said, "My name is Lucas. Nice to meet you, Jamal. In my dreams, I can fly." Jamal nodded and shook his hand.

The next and final person to step up caught Jamal by complete surprise. He thought she was stunningly beautiful. She had a mocha-brown complexion, hair was straight but cut extremely close to her head. Her eyebrows were expertly groomed and arched, which framed the sharpest azure-blue eyes he had ever seen, let alone on a person of color. He wanted to say, *"Girl, you are fierce!"* but he kept his thoughts to himself.

"Hi, Jamal. My name is Keira. In my dreams I have the gift of camouflage, which for all intents and purposes, turns me invisible."

"Nice to meet you, Keira," Jamal said. "Nice to meet you all. As far as I can tell, I don't have special abilities like the rest of you in my dreams. My dreams are more like nightmares. For the past few weeks, I've been stalked and until last night I wasn't sure what it was."

"What did it turn out to be?" Lucas asked.

Jamal hesitated, which prompted Dr. Garcia to say, "It's okay, Jamal. You can tell them."

Jamal took a sharp breath inward and slowly exhaled before quietly stating, "It's a werewolf."

For the second time that morning, he was caught by surprise as his fellow dream participants' eyes lit up like Christmas Trees. They appeared to be excited.

Dr. Garcia smiled and handed Jamal the clipboard with the consent form and a pen. He said, "I think you have your answer, Mr. Robinson."

While Jamal accepted and began to sign the form, Dr. Garcia turned and gave a thumbs up sign to his colleagues, Dr.'s Perez and Miller, who gave each other high-fives before stepping out of the room they were in to have a private chat in the hallway.

Filled with glee, Dr. Perez said, "Do you know what this means?"

Dr. Miller, just as elated said, "Yes, this could be the breakthrough that we've been waiting for!"

At that moment, Tank was heading back from the restroom when he saw the doctors talking excitedly in the hallway. They hadn't seen him yet, so he ducked into the opening of an adjacent room so that he could eavesdrop on their conversation.

"Just think," Dr. Perez was saying, "The possibilities are endless. If this works, we could pull real money from the bank vaults in dreams and fund our own research. No more scrounging for grants and donations! We'll be self-funded!"

"Yes," Dr. Miller said, "And the test subjects are already briefed and ready for action. If they pull this off, they know they will be paid handsomely, and it will be the start of a beautiful partnership but what of the latest addition?"

"Well, he's unaware that he's just a pawn to test our groups' abilities in the field. There's also no point in telling him that their dream abilities are also real-world abilities."

Puzzled, Tank thought, *What the fuck are they talking about? Real world abilities? So, they're not really interested in helping Jamal with his nightmares? They're just using him. Oh, hell no! I've got to put an end to this bullshit and get my baby out of here!*

By the time Tank came out of hiding, however, the doctors had already gone back into the observation room. He ran into the room to see that all four sleep participants were already in a prone position in adjoining beds and hooked up to all kinds of electronic gadgetry.

Jamal was the last in the row, and Dr. Garcia was removing a needle from his arm.

"What did he just give him?" Tank demanded.

Dr. Perez turned and said, "Please try and calm down. It's just a sedative to help induce REM sleep."

"Well, I need you to wake him back the hell up. We're not doing this. I'm taking Jamal home."

"I'm afraid it's too late for that," Dr. Miller said. "Besides, Jamal already provided his consent."

"Where is this coming from, Tank?" asked Dr. Perez. "Just a few short minutes ago you were all for this."

"That was before I heard you two assholes talking! You're not interested in helping Jamal. You're just using him as a test subject for your three lackeys in there!"

"How unfortunate!" said Dr. Garcia as he entered the room brandishing a gun. "If you two idiots are done flapping your gums, please tie up our guest securely in a chair."

Tank was about to put up a fight, but Dr. Garcia said, "I would cooperate if I were you. Make one wrong move and I'll shoot you in the kneecap and then I'll shoot your Boo in the head. It would be an unfortunate turn of events, but the show must go on. Now, it's your move!"

Fuming, Tank sat obediently in a chair while Dr. Miller tied his hands behind his back and Dr. Perez tied his feet to the legs of the chair.

Now smiling, Dr. Garcia put his gun in one of his lab coat pockets. He then moved to stand in front of Tank. He bent down until he was at eye level and said, "Now, are we going to have to gag you too? Or are you going to keep quiet and enjoy the show?"

Tank resisted the urge to spit in the doctor's face. Instead, he gritted his teeth and glared at Dr. Garcia, which seemed to please the evil man.

"Excellent choice! Now let's all sit back and enjoy the show. Our participants are all beyond exhausted so it shouldn't be much longer now." He then took a seat and looked at Dr. Miller. "Henry, do you mind getting the lights?"

Dr. Miller turned the lights to both rooms off and then he joined his colleagues at the console facing the monitors and the adjoining room where the four test subjects were now sleeping.

Tank took advantage of the darkness of the room and the fact that the physicians now had their backs to him to quietly begin working on his bonds.

Dr. Perez pointed to one of the monitors and said, "Hey, I think something's happening!"

All eyes were glued to the monitor in question as a night sky illuminated the screen, followed by a rolling fog. It seemed to disperse quickly to reveal a full silver moon and an open field with majestic mountains in the background.

In the middle of the field was a massive two-hundred-foot tree that appeared to be full of black leaves. The stars from above seemed to be captured amongst the leaves as there were twinkling lights that resembled LED lights providing an additional light source.

It wasn't long before a female came walking into the frame. She was dressed in black leather with holsters and a harness that seemed to carry all sorts of weaponry. Her hair was pulled tight into a braided ponytail that touched her butt.

"Hey! That's Nadia!" Dr. Perez said. "It's working! This is working!"

From what could be seen on screen, she was carrying guns, knives, grenades, and a sword. She turned to the left and you could see the skyline of a city off in the distance. As she started walking towards the city, she suddenly looked up to see that Lucas was coming in for a landing.

He landed beside her wearing blue jeans, a white t-shirt, and sneakers. His hair was neatly combed, and he looked rather handsome. He smiled at Nadia and the pair started to walk off together but Lucas appeared to bump into something that neither he nor Nadia could see.

It was at this point that a smiling Keira revealed herself. She was wearing a powder blue summer dress with matching sneakers. She said something to Nadia and Lucas and the three of them just laughed and laughed.

"Damn!" Dr. Garcia said as he slapped the console. "I wish we could have figured out how to account for sound!"

"Hey!" Dr. Perez said. "I agree it sucks that we can't hear any dialogue but are you fucking kidding me? Look at what we've managed to accomplish! We are viewing and recording dreams! Not only that but shared dreams! We did that!"

Dr. Miller then chimed in by saying, "And that's just the tip of the iceberg!"

Meanwhile, Tank, still busy with loosening his bonds and making some progress, was worried about Jamal. He continued watching the monitors hoping and praying that they would both make it out of this mess somehow.

Once Nadia, Lucas and Keira were closer to the city limits, a fourth figure could be seen. It wasn't long before all concerned parties recognized Jamal. Unlike the other dreamers though, Jamal hadn't changed clothes. He was still wearing his hospital gown and he appeared to be in pain as he fell to the ground.

"What's wrong with him?" Nadia asked.

"I have no idea," Keira said as she knelt down and laid the back side of her right hand against his forehead. "Oh my GOD!" she said, standing up. "He's burning up!"

Jamal suddenly cried out and started vibrating.

While the doctors were riveted to the monitors, Tank was paying attention to the actual people who were asleep in the adjacent room. He panicked once he saw Jamal start to subtly vibrate.

"Hey!" He suddenly yelled, "Fuck your so-called experiment! Something is seriously wrong! Jamal is vibrating in the sleep study room!"

"Will you please just shut the fuck up!" Dr. Garcia said. "He's dreaming, you idiot! He's acting out his dream!"

Tank was about to protest further, but the things that were happening on the monitors caught his attention. Jamal began to contort as he continued to yell out in apparent pain. He rolled over from his back to his hands and knees and his back began to arch and elongate.

The flesh seemed to erupt and sprout fur. His face stretched along with his mouth, nose, and ears to resemble the snout of a wolf. His eyes turned from a dark brown to the color of amber. His arms and legs morphed as well. When all was said and done, Jamal was a whopping seven feet tall, standing on the hind legs of a wolf and loomed over the relatively small in comparison figures of Nadia, Lucas, and Keira.

Dr. Perez stood up from his seat and said, "Holy mother of GOD! He wasn't being stalked. He is the motherfucking werewolf!"

A tear slowly trailed from Tank's left eye as he saw that his beloved boyfriend had transitioned into this creature in real life as well, still asleep in the dream catcher room next to the clueless other participants. The doctors still had no idea, as they were fixated on the monitors.

Finally, Tank was able to free his hands and with the doctors still otherwise engaged, he went to work on freeing his legs.

Returning to the dreamland, Keira went into Camouflage mode, while Lucas took flight. Nadia stood her ground and went into attack mode. She pulled two guns and fired repeatedly into the torso of the werewolf. The attack did not produce the desired effect, serving only to annoy the creature instead. Jamal, slash the werewolf swiftly backhanded Nadia, sending her flying backwards.

She somersaulted and landed on her feet. Screaming a war cry, she charged forward while snatching a grenade from her uniform. She pulled the pin with her teeth and launched the weapon forward towards the werewolf's face.

The creature caught the grenade, grabbed Nadia by the throat and stuffed the live grenade in her mouth. Seconds later, it went off, obliterating her head. Simultaneously, the sleeping body of Nadia suffered the same fate. Brain matter and bits of skull painted the walls of the sleep study room.

The doctors were still glued to the monitors, but Tank was focused on the room where the participants were sleeping. The moment Nadia's head exploded he screamed, "Holy shit! Holy fucking shit! She's dead! This shit is real! Get him out! Pull him out of the fucking dream!"

The doctors finally listened and looked into the room of the sleeping participants. They were all shocked to see that Nadia was just as dead in real life as she was in the dreamscape. They also began freaking out once they noticed that the body of Jamal also resembled the werewolf from the monitors.

Dr. Perez was the first to speak. "Okay, I think under the circumstances we need to abort and regroup. We did not consider that a fucking werewolf could be the real deal. We need to pull them out of the dream before things get even worse."

"To hell we will!" Dr. Garcia said, "We wanted to test our subjects, well, here is the ultimate test!"

"Come on, Jeffrey!" Dr. Miller said, "We've just lost one of our subjects, for Christ's sake!"

While the doctors continued to argue amongst themselves, Tank took the opportunity to free his feet. He tried to remain calm and think of his next steps when he realized that the monitors had gone blank and the surviving members of the dreamscape were starting to wake up in the adjoining room, including Jamal, who was still in full on werewolf mode. And he was stirring awake.

Panicking, Dr. Garcia ran to the door to the adjoining room and locked it just as Keira and Lucas tried to escape. They pleaded and banged on the door to be released but Dr. Garcia simply nodded no and backed away.

Tank seized the opportunity. He snatched the keys from Dr. Garcia's hands and grabbed his badge to boot. He exited the room and locked the doctors inside just as Jamal the werewolf eased off his bed and lumbered forward.

Lucas immediately flew up towards the ceiling and hovered there while Keira went into camouflage mode, backing away from the door.

Dr. Garcia fumbled for his gun, pulled it from his lab coat and aimed it at Tank's head. "You have ten seconds to unlock that door and let us out," he said. "Or I will blow your motherfucking brains out!"

Tank simply smiled, gave the terrified doctor the middle finger and pointed behind him. Dr. Garcia began to tremble as he heard glass breaking behind him. The next thing he felt was powerful jaws tearing and ripping into his neck and shoulder. He barely had time to scream as his life's blood began to paint the room.

Not knowing what else to do, Tank ran for the elevators. Dr. Miller screamed, "No! Please don't leave us!" But Tank ignored his cries for help and kept going. He could hear Dr. Miller's screams get even louder as the werewolf began to tear him apart limb from limb. He made it the elevator banks and pressed the up button.

Just as the loan elevator arrived, Tank heard more glass breaking. He looked to his left to see that Dr. Perez must have dived headfirst through the glass door. He was scrambling to his feet and headed Tank's way just as the car opened.

"You're not leaving me down here you cocksucker!" Dr. Perez yelled.

Tank quickly swiped the stolen badge underneath the floor buttons and pressed first-floor as soon as the scan turned green. The elevator doors managed to close in Dr. Perez' face not a moment too soon. He could hear the doctor cursing and pounding on the doors as he went up.

Back inside the observation room, Lucas, still sticking close to the ceiling, tried to fly out and into the hallway. He was not expecting the werewolf to leap straight up and snatch him right out of the air. The creature bit through his neck so hard, he was instantly decapitated.

Upon reaching the first floor, Tank quickly exited the elevator and ran to the receptionist's desk. He knew he looked like a crazed nutjob, but he didn't care. Everyone had to be warned. "I need you to listen very carefully to me," he began. You must call security. You need to shut down all the elevators and you need to evacuate the building.

The receptionist was understandably alarmed but guarded just the same. "I'm sorry sir, but on whose authority? And who are you?" she asked.

"I'm the guy that's trying to save your life! Dr. Garcia is dead. A patient he and Dr. Miller and Dr. Perez were working with is dead! They were doing fucking dream experiments and now there's a fucking werewolf on the loose. My boyfriend! He's…"

Tank couldn't finish. Everything that he had just experienced hit him all at once. The reality of it all was just too much to bear. He collapsed in front of the receptionists' desk and began to weep.

That was all the receptionist needed. She quickly grabbed her phone and dialed for security, instructing them to come to the lobby asap to deal with an emergency.

Meanwhile, back in the basement, Keira, still under camouflage, eased into the hallway and headed for the stairwell. She saw that Dr. Perez had given up on the elevator and was headed for them as well. When she heard the werewolf leave the observation room and heard the crunching of glass underneath its' feet, she stopped moving. She plastered herself against the wall and held her breath as the creature started to move pass her.

Suddenly, it stopped. Its nostrils flared in and out and then it turned its' head and appeared to look right at her. Her heart just about stopped, and she was on the verge of pissing herself when the elevator dinged and opened its doors. This drew the creature's attention and it loped off towards it at a quick gallop. Keira dropped the camouflage and doubled over and grasped her knees as she forced herself to breathe again.

Dr. Perez heard the elevator and ran for it. He saw Keira but did not see the creature anywhere, so he entered the car. He thought for a hot second to call out to Keira then thought better of it. "She can fend for herself," he thought. He scanned his badge and hit the button for the first floor. Once the elevator doors closed, he breathed a sigh of relief and leaned against the wall and closed his eyes.

He reached up to touch his face when he felt something dripping on it, which caused him to open his eyes. Clinging above him in the elevator car was the werewolf. It was its drool that was dripping on him. Dr. Perez screamed as it descended upon him and began tearing him apart, limb from limb.

The sounds of devastation could be heard in the lobby of the building as the elevator reached the first floor. Tank pulled himself off the floor just as a team of security officers rushed past him. Once he was upright, he looked at the receptionist with tears in his eyes and said, "Get out and get out now while you still can!" He then turned and bolted through the lobby doors and out into the street.

The confused receptionist watched Tank leave, but her attention was then drawn back to the elevators and the security guards. As the doors to the elevator opened, the werewolf step outside it and growled with the blood of Dr. Perez still dripping from its maws.

All Tank could hear as he ran down the street was screams and gunshots. Final destination unknown.

Stop the Madness

It was a hot and sultry summer evening in Philadelphia. The night was thriving with throngs of people roaming here and there without a care in the world. Everyone was in a good mood and full of life with excitement and anticipation of the next day's Fourth of July festivities.

Four friends sat down at a popular diner in the Northern Liberties section of town, located on the four hundred block of Spring Garden Street.

Jasmine was cute and petite with light brown skin and blue-black hair cut into a pixie style. Straight and close on the sides, with a wavy volume of curls up top. She was wearing denim cutoff shorts with a thin, black tank top.

Katrina has a darker skin tone and aside from the cinnamon-red coloring, kept her hair in its natural state of curls that crowned her head resembling a weeping willow tree the way it framed her face. She has an athletic build but rarely shows off her body. This evening was no exception as she opted for an untucked pale blue t-shirt and a pair of jeans.

Leonard, a little above average height at an even six feet has a dark brown complexion and was in body builder shape. His hair was close to his head and wavy with a bald fade on the sides. He also sported a well-groomed beard. He was dressed in all black, t-shirt, jeans and sneakers.

Malcolm was dark-skinned, with a stocky physique and stood at five-foot ten inches. His hair was also cut close on the sides and back, but he has twisted dreads on top that were about three inches in length. He was wearing a red, graphic t-shirt and blue jeans.

This diner is one of their favorite hang-out spots. Known for its chrome exterior with neon green lighting and retro-style interior, the cuisine served is by far the main attraction. Awarded four and a half stars, the food is considered by many to be miles above standard diner food fare.

A waitress arrived almost immediately and handed out menus to the new arrivals. "Good evening! Welcome to Emerald City. My name is Alison and I'll be your server. Can I get you all something to drink to get started?"

Jasmine responded first, "I'll have a blood orange margarita please."

Katrina said, "I'll try the Purple Rain. It sounds good!"

Leonard responded next, "I'll have a Stella, please."

The waitress looked at Malcolm and asked, "And what would you like to drink young man?"

Smiling, he said, "I think I'm gonna go with a Blue Moon."

Alison tapped her pen on her pad and said, "Great, four drinks coming right up." Shen then left the foursome to put their beverage order in.

"Okay," Jasmine said to the table. "What on the menu looks good to you guys?"

"I think I'm going to have the roasted beet salad," Katrina said.

"Gross! Leonard said. I'm going for the spicy buffalo chicken wings."

"And what's your problem with beets?" Katrina asked.

Leonard threw up his hands and said, "Hey, no offense. To each his own and all that. I just don't like the taste of 'em." He shook his head and made a face as if he currently had a piece in his mouth.

"Katrina laughed and said, "You are too funny! What about you Malcolm?"

"You know me! I can never pass up a burger and fries! Jasmine, what about you?"

"I think I'm going to go with the disco fries. They are calling my name with that braised short rib they put on top of them. Yes, LAWD and no, I'm not sharing!"

The friends all laughed and gathered their menus so the waitress could grab them at one time. She arrived with their drinks, took their food orders, and left the table again.

Two guys then walked past the group and one of them locked eyes with Leonard and gave him a slight smile and a nod. He was tall and fit, with dirty blonde hair. Leonard smiled back but noticed that the other guy didn't look so good, as if he might be sick. He was a lot shorter, maybe five foot eight, with jet black hair. The pair sat at the booth directly behind Leonard and his friends.

Malcolm noticed the subtle exchange but kept his thoughts to himself. He returned his attention to Jasmine and asked, "Hey, where's your man, Sean? I thought he was meeting us here?"

Jasmine frowned and said, "He texted me and said he was being held up at work. He's going to try and catch up with us later. He said he'd call once he's finally done for the night. What about you and Sheila? What's going on with you two? We haven't seen her for a minute."

Malcolm suddenly put his face in his hands. Before his now concerned friends could react, he looked at them all with tears in his eyes and said, "We're done. I caught her stepping out with some other dude a few weeks back."

"What?" Katrina asked. "I don't believe it! She loves you! You two are magic together!"

"Yeah," Malcolm responded. "I thought so too! That's why I purchased this." Malcolm reached into his pocket and pulled out a black velvet box and sat it on the table.

"Oh...my...GOD!" Jasmine said. "Is that..."

Malcolm opened the box to show his friends a three stone oval cut diamond engagement ring.

Leonard touched his friend on the shoulder and said, "Oh, man! I'm so sorry dude!"

"Wait a minute!" Katrina said. "Back it up a bit. Tell us what happened. How do you know for sure that she was cheating on you?"

"I was coming out of Jeweler's Row after purchasing this," Malcolm began as he grabbed the box and put it back in his pocket. "I walked up to Market Street, and I saw Sheila coming out of the Fashion District Mall. She was hanging all over this dude's arm and they were laughing and carrying on as if they were having the time of their lives."

"What did you do?" Jasmine asked. "Did you confront them?"

"I sure as hell did! I ran across the street as if my ass was on fire! My intent was to beat the living shit out of that motherfucker but after a brief and heated exchange, I realized that the brutha had no idea that I even existed, so I backed off."

"And what about Sheila?" Leonard asked. "Did she even try to explain herself?"

"She was crying and damn near hysterical at being busted. If she did try to explain herself, I couldn't hear it. I was so upset and disgusted with her that I left her standing there on the corner. I think the dude that she was with left her as well. And before any of you ask, no, I haven't spoken with her since and I don't intend on talking to that bitch ever again. Matter of fact, I blocked her number."

Jasmine said, "Normally, I would say that's a bit harsh, but under the circumstances, I completely get where you're coming from. I'm so sorry Malcolm. I wish that I'd known about this sooner."

"Why, what could you have done?"

"No, it's not what I could have done. It's what I did."

Everyone at the same time asked, "What are you talking about? What did you do?"

"Please don't kill me. You must understand that I didn't know. I had no idea."

"Just spit it out Jasmine," Malcolm said. "What did you do?"

Jasmine inhaled deeply, exhaled, and blurted out, "I told Sheila we would be here tonight and asked her to join us!"

"No, you did not!" Malcolm said as he leaned back and looked towards the ceiling.

"Well, maybe she won't show," Katrina said. "She knows she fucked up a good thing, so maybe she's off licking her wounds or something."

"I… don't think so." Leonard said, causing everyone to give him a quizzical look. He nodded his head in the direction of the door to the diner and said, "She just walked in."

Standing in the entrance and looking around the diner was Sheila wearing a white ruffled mini dress with thin spaghetti straps and white sneakers. Light-skinned with dark auburn hair that touched her shoulders styled in big, wavy curls, she looked stunningly beautiful.

Everyone turned to face the entrance and quickly returned to their previous positions. Malcolm stared daggers at Jasmine, who grimaced, threw up her hands and said, "I'm sorry!"

"On that note," Leonard said as he eased out of the booth. "This is my cue to take a piss. I did not order a side of drama to go with my wings." As he stood up completely, Sheila arrived at the booth. "Oh, hey, Sheila!" Leonard said. "Bye, Sheila." He then quickly made his way towards the men's room.

"Hey, Leonard!" Sheila said. She then turned her attention to the rest of the group. "Hey girls. Jasmine, thanks for inviting me. Malcolm, can we talk?"

After a quick frustrated glance at Jasmine, Malcolm said, "Yeah, let's talk."

As he eased out of the booth, Jasmine silently mouthed the words, "I'm sorry."

Malcolm frowned and said, "Don't any of you dare touch my fries! I'll be right back." He then ushered Sheila out of the diner so they could talk in private.

Katrina turned to face Jasmine and said, "Girl, what were you thinking? Malcolm is pissed!"

"How was I supposed to know they had broken up? Did you know?"

Katrina twisted her lips and said, "No. Just like you I had no idea. I was completely shocked."

At that moment, the dirty blonde guy in the next booth got up and headed for the men's room. When he entered, Leonard was at the sink washing his hands.

"Hey, Alan!" Leonard said as he grabbed a few paper napkins to dry his hands. "I thought you had other plans this evening."

"I did but my buddy Sloan had some kind of accident at work."

"Is that the guy you came in here with?"

"Yeah, that's him."

"Well, I hate to tell you this man but he's not looking to good."

"I know but he refuses to go to the hospital."

"What happened to him if you don't mind me asking?"

"That's the thing. The way he tells it, it wasn't anything serious. He works at that research facility in University City. He was placing one of the lab rats back in its' cage when it bit him. He cleaned and dressed the wound, ended his shift, and met up with me." A look suddenly came over Alan's face as he remembered something.

"Hey, what is it?"

"It's the weirdest thing. When I met up with Sloan, he was his normal jovial self, but I'm telling you, five minutes went by, and he doubled over in pain."

"Really?"

"Yeah, I asked him what was wrong, and he said he was having the most intense hunger pains he's ever experienced. When I suggested I take him to the hospital, he insisted that he just needed something to eat. That's when I remembered you asked me to meet you here."

"Well, I'm flattered, but maybe you should get back out there and check on him."

"I will but not before I do what I came in here to do."

"Oh, yeah? What's that?"

"This," Alan said as he grabbed Leonard, pulled him in close and planted a long and passionate kiss on his lips."

After a minute, Alan released Leonard and headed for the door. "Are you coming?" he asked, as Leonard smiled and followed him out of the bathroom.

As they returned to their respective booths, Alan became immediately alarmed once he saw Sloan slumped over in his seat. He yelled out his buddy's name and began violently shaking him.

Leonard came over and said, "Hey, is everything okay?"

"No! Dear sweet Jesus! I think he's dead! He's cold as ice and unresponsive."

Leonard pulled out his phone and said, "Try to check his pulse. I'm going to call 911."

Before he could though, another patron in the diner suddenly yelled, "Hey, there's something happening on the news! Turn up the volume!"

Everyone's eyes were glued to the television as one of the waitresses turned up the volume. The images displayed were showing people in the streets running around and violently attacking each other while a reporter proceeded to give commentary on the situation.

"Good evening. This is Chet Huntley reporting live for WBAC in front of the Scientific Research Facility in University City. I have standing here beside me one of the directors of animal research, Dr. Judy Baum. Dr. Baum, as the police try to contain the situation before us, can you tell us what's happening right now and what this has to do with your facility?"

Dr. Baum appeared ready to jump out of her skin. Her eyes were constantly darting around as if she feared for her safety. "All I can tell you is that one of our employees was conducting unsanctioned experiments on a few of the animals. We are not completely sure on all the details just yet but when it was discovered he was immediately fired. He managed to break free from the security detail attempting to escort him from the building."

"Do you know what this employee did next?"

"Yes, he somehow made it back to his lab and released all the animals that were under his care. Unfortunately, we had to put them down, the ones that we could find, as they all exhibited signs of rabies."

"So, are you saying that these people running around attacking without provocation is a result of rabies?"

"No, Chet. I'm afraid it's worse than that."

"I'm sorry. Worse than rabies? What do you mean?"

"This is going to be hard for your viewers to digest so I'll keep it as simple as I can. If you are bitten, in a matter of five to ten minutes you will experience the most intense pain of hunger and then..." The doctor hesitated to continue.

"And then what, Dr. Baum?"

"And then you die."

Katrina and Jasmine gasped and got up from the booth to stand next to Leonard.

Katrina said, "Did she just say that you die?"

Leonard looked at her and nodded his head yes, then returned his attention to the television.

The reporter Chet's eyes opened wide as he continued his interview, "I'm sorry Dr. Baum. If it's true that you die after being bitten, how do you account for the perpetrators randomly attacking people?"

"My best guess is that they are somehow reanimated as a result of the experiments of our former employee."

"Are you trying to tell us that... that these people are zombies?"

"For all intents and purposes... Yes! Now, I'm sorry but I am fearing for my safety, and you should too. Tell your viewers that they need to keep themselves and their loved ones behind locked and closed doors until this situation is contained. I'm afraid I must be going now."

"I can expect that Dr. Baum but before I let you go, do the police know who they are looking for? Can you give us the name of the suspected instigator of all this?"

"I sure can and yes, the police have the name and picture of our former employee. His name is Sloan Chancellor. You should avoid contact at all costs and contact the police immediately!"

The doctor than abruptly walked off camera. The waitress turned the volume down as Leonard and Alan quickly looked at each other and then the booth his friend was in. Sloan was no longer there but was instead standing right next to Alan looking like death warmed over. His eyes were completely white, as if the pupils had rolled to the back of his head. He then lunged for Alan and tried to bite him.

"Oh, shit!" Leonard said as he took a quick step backwards.

Katrina and Jasmine screamed as Alan and Sloan fell to the floor, causing the rest of the diner patrons to take notice. Alan did his best to keep out of reach of Sloan's attempts to bite him.

Leonard threw his right leg back as if he were about to punt in a football game. He kicked Sloan as hard as he could, his foot connecting with the dead man's head sending him flying backwards and off Alan. He quickly reached down to give Alan a hand and helped him back to his feet.

"Are you okay? Did he bite you?"

"No and thanks, by the way. I'm fine."

Just then they heard a woman scream. Sloan was tearing at her neck like a dog with a bone. He let her fall to the floor and then placed his sights back on Alan. Before he could move though his head exploded into smithereens from the blast of a shotgun. Everyone turned to see the cook coming from around the counter with the weapon.

"Everyone okay out here?" he asked.

Jasmine and Katrina, clearly traumatized, were hugging each other but nodded their heads yes when he looked at them. Just then Malcolm and Sheila entered the diner. The cook spun around and pointed his weapon at them.

Malcom and Sheila threw their hands up and Malcolm said, "Yo! What the hell's going on in here?"

The cook lowered his weapon and walked over to the doors and locked it. He then said, "I'm sorry but we just had some lunatic attacking people. He just killed that poor woman over there, so I had to take him out."

"What?" Malcolm asked as he looked to where the cook was pointing and said, "Jesus! Don't look Sheila!"

Alice, the waitress said, "The police are on their way, so everybody please sit tight."

"To hell with that noise!" one of the patrons said. "I'm getting the hell out of here!"

"Yeah! Me too!" Someone else said and people started moving towards the exit.

The cook put his back to the door and cocked his weapon, causing the people wanting to leave to stop dead in their tracks and then someone screamed again, pointing towards the windows by the booths. All attention went to the windows and there was a collective gasp as there were nothing but several faces of the dead peering in at them.

The reanimated began pounding on the glass until it started cracking. With all attention focused on the windows, no one noticed the dead woman with the chewed-out neck suddenly sit up.

The Cemetery

It's an unusually warm spring night for April in southwest Philadelphia as five friends make their way to the entrance of Mount Peace Cemetery. Forgotten and abandoned, the place is slowly being reclaimed by the forest it was once built on.

Expanding nearly 400 acres, it opened in eighteen fifty-five, boasting an ornate Romanesque entrance and gothic mausoleums. Now decrepit and lying-in ruins, it is mostly overgrown with weeds, toppled over headstones and resembles a gothic fairytale.

"Who the hell thought it would be fun to hold a party in a cemetery?" asked Jerome, the tallest of the group at six feet, two inches. He had caramel-brown smooth skin, straight white teeth and cut short curly black hair with a bald fade and neatly trimmed beard. His brown eyes were so dark they could almost be mistaken for black.

Jerome was usually an even-tempered, mellow dude but as soon as they got to the entrance, he felt a chill go up his spine and began to have second thoughts about proceeding any further.

Belinda spun around so fast that her black mini skirt flared up almost high enough to expose the fact that she wasn't wearing any underwear. Beautiful, busty and headstrong, her shoulder-length black weave bristled behind her as she briskly walked up to get in Jerome's face.

Her light-skinned, even complexion seemed to glow as brightly as the red lipstick she was wearing. She jammed an index finger into Jerome's chest and said, "You did not bring us all the way out here just to chicken out now, did you?"

At five-foot, seven, it was an odd sight to see her step to this tall man so aggressively, but Jerome just laughed it off and said, "Calm down, okay? I'm just saying it's a peculiar place for a good time."

"He's right babe," said Derrick as he threw an arm around Belinda's shoulders. "It's creepy as hell, and I for one am not going to be dancing on some poor soul's grave." He took a swig of tequila from the bottle he was holding as Belinda threw his arm from around her.

She thought about something smart to say but as she looked at Derrick's dark five-foot ten-inch muscular frame, head full of short sponge twists, brown eyes, full lips and goatee, she just snatched the tequila bottle from his hands, let out a heavy sigh and turned to Cassie.

"Girl, help me out with these two would you please?" She then took a swig for herself before handing the bottle back to Derrick.

Cassie, all of five eight with a slim runner's build and cropped cinnamon-red hair stepped closer to the group and said, "Guys, you know Jackie's a little cuckoo for coco puffs and thinks that she's some goddammed witch or voodoo priestess or some-such shit. Anyway, it's her birthday and this is where she wanted to celebrate it. You all agreed to come so let's get this over with."

Belinda then looked at Patrick. Patrick is clean shaven and an even six feet, with a tight, muscular body with green eyes, olive skin and dark brown hair trimmed neatly on the sides with a part. Everyone says he looks like he belongs on the runways of New York, Paris and Milan.

"What?" he asked, throwing up his hands. "I didn't say a word."

"Exactly," Belinda said. "You've been mighty quiet this whole time. Do you have anything to add?"

"Only that I have to pee! So, let's get this show on the road so I can find a tree or something."

Everyone laughed and they then proceeded through the crumbling entrance. After a few minutes of walking, Jerome asked, "So, how are we supposed to find them again?"

Cassie responded, "Jackie said to stay on the path from the entrance and we'll know when we've arrived."

"Well, shit!" Derrick said. "Ominous much?"

"Alright guys," Patrick said. "I see a tree with my name on it. You all go on ahead of me and I'll catch up with you."

"Don't be long," Belinda said. "We'd hate for you to get lost out here in the dark!"

Patrick simply waved her off and ran towards the tree without saying another word. He let out a huge sigh of relief as he relieved himself. When that was done, he zipped himself up and was about to head back towards the path when he realized a rather handsome, middle-aged black man with salt and pepper hair walking towards him.

"Holy shit!" He thought to himself, trying not to panic. He was trying to decide if he should run or stand his ground but then the stranger just waved and smiled.

"Sorry son," The stranger said. "I didn't mean to startle you but what are you doing out here?"

Swallowing hard, Patrick decided to be honest with the stranger. "A friend of mine is having a party out here to celebrate her birthday. We're not breaking any laws, are we? We thought this place was abandoned."

"What's your name son?"

"Uh, Patrick?"

The stranger extended his hand and said, "Well, nice to meet you, Patrick. I'm Myles Chesterbrook. No, you're not breaking any laws, but don't you think it's rather inappropriate? This place may be abandoned but there are still people buried out here."

Patrick reciprocated the handshake gesture and said, "I didn't realize that. I don't think my friends did either. We certainly don't mean any disrespect to the dead."

Myles' smile faded and a serious look came across his face as he said, "You seem like a genuinely sincere, forthright young man. I want you to take what I'm about to say seriously. You need to grab your friends and get out of here as quickly as possible. Spirits are real and some of them are really, really angry about being dead. That's nothing you want to play around with. You see that full moon?"

Patrick looked up at the glowing satellite with the slightly pink glow. He returned his gaze to Myles and slowly nodded yes.

"That's what's called a 'Supermoon'. On nights like tonight, the spirits are at their strongest and the dead can walk the earth."

Just then Patrick felt a hand clamp down on his shoulder. He yelled out and spun around to see Jerome standing there. "Jerome! He said, "What the hell are you doing sneaking up on me like that. You scared the living shit out of me!"

"Hey," Jerome said. "I'm sorry. I didn't mean to startle you but who are you talking to?"

Patrick made a gesture and turned as he said, "What do you mean? I'm talking to…" but when he turned around Myles was nowhere to be found. "What the…? He was just here! Didn't you see him?"

"See who?"

"Myles! He said his name was Myles Chesterbrook!"

Jerome kind of gave Patrick the side-eye as he said, "Are you fucking with me? I didn't see anyone here besides you as I walked up."

"Dammit, I'm not making this up and I'm not crazy. He came up to me just as soon as I finished pissing and basically said we shouldn't be here partying because the dead are still buried here."

"Ok. Well, maybe he saw me coming and took off."

Patrick shook his head and began to massage the back of his neck as he looked around one last time. He said, "Yeah, maybe. What are you doing here anyway? Did you think I was lost?"

"No. But I did want to speak with you alone and apologize. Belinda was right. During the whole trip out here, you never said a word. I know you're still mad at me."

"I'm not mad," Patrick said. "I'm disappointed. I'm hurt. You hurt me! When we got together that wasn't just sex for me. I finally felt comfortable enough to tell you how I felt but when I told you that I loved you, you bolted! Do you have any idea how that made me feel? I felt like a complete fucking idiot!"

"I am so sorry. I know I could've handled that better. It's no excuse but you caught me completely off guard. Please believe me when I say I never intended to hurt you. This is all new to me. Never in a million years did I imagine that I would fall in love with a man. You kind of snuck up on me and I didn't know how to handle that, my emotions I mean."

"Wait, what? You love me?"

"Yes! That's what I'm trying to tell you, you fucking idiot!" Jerome laughed. "I don't even like Jackie! You're the only reason I agreed to come to this insanely bullshit party of hers."

A single tear slowly made its' way down Patrick's cheek as he said, "I don't... I don't know what to say."

"You don't have to say anything," Jerome said as he pulled Patrick into an embrace and kissed him passionately.

After a moment, and hand in hand, the two then slowly made their way back towards the path.   "Wait," Patrick said as he lifted their hands in the air. "Are we arriving like this, or should we keep it chill and low-key, just between us?"

Smiling, Jerome said, "I'm not ashamed, are you?"

"No," Patrick said as he returned the smile and lowered their hands back. The two then proceeded briskly up the path to catch up to the rest of their friends.

When they finally arrived at the designated spot, the party was in full swing with music blaring and what looked like at least fifty partygoers dancing and drinking the night away.

Swaying dreamily with her eyes closed, there was Jackie, the party girl herself dancing alone on top of a tree stump taking gulps from a bottle of Veuve Clicquot Champagne. Her hair was in an upswept do, with curling tendrils framing her face. Her dress was red and gold sporting a flared, knee-length skirt.

She definitely seemed to be enjoying the celebration of her twenty-fifth, oblivious to the fact that her boyfriend Daniel was eyeing another partygoer. Up against a tree behind her were Belinda and Derrick, who were making out.

The pair then spotted Cassie heading towards them with a light-skinned black man in tow. Upon reaching them, she grabbed their hands and then reached up to kiss each of them on the cheek.

"I don't know what's going on or when this happened, but I approve and I adore you both!" she said, taking a step back. "By the way, this is Michael," she stated, gesturing to the handsome stranger.   "Michael, this is Jerome, and this is Patrick. They are two of my best friends."

Michael extended his hand and said, "It's nice to meet you both. How long have you been together?"

Patrick and Jerome exchanged a quick glance before Jerome said, "It's nice to meet you as well. We just made it official tonight, I guess."

"Well then, congratulations! This calls for a toast! Drinks are on me!" Michael turned to Cassie and said, "What can I get you beautiful?"

"If the boys don't object, I think this moment more than calls for some champagne." Jerome and Patrick nodded their approval and Michael left without another word to fetch the drinks.

With an incredulous look on her face, Cassie said, "I don't even know where to begin. I mean I had no idea that you two... I have so many questions!"

Jerome laughed and told her they'd be willing to answer them all, but this was not the time, nor the place.

She opened her mouth to protest but Michael reappeared with the cups of champagne and handed them out. Once everyone had a drink in their hand, he raised his cup and said, "I want to wish you both a long lasting and happy, healthy relationship. Cheers!"

The small group reciprocated the cheers sentiment, and each took a sip from their prospective cups. Everyone was all smiles until Patrick dropped his cup with a look of terror on his face. The color seemed to drain from his face as he pointed a shaky finger at a nearby headstone.

"Patrick?" Cassie asked. "Are you trying to scare me?"

"Babe?" Said a now concerned Jerome. "What is it? What are you pointing at?"

"We have to get out of here and we have to get out of here now!" Patrick exclaimed as he went to stand in front of the headstone he had been pointing at.

Everyone gathered around him to read the headstone, which read; Myles Chesterbrook, Beloved Son, Father and Brother. Sunrise 1942 – Sunset 1998.

Confused, Jerome said, "I don't understand."

"Don't you see," Patrick said, unable to keep the panic out of his voice. "This is the man who came to me by the tree. The man you said you didn't see but I had a full-fledged conversation with!"

"Jerome," Cassie said. "What's he talking about?"

"When I left you guys to go look for him, I found him standing by a tree. It looked to me like he was talking to himself, but he said some guy named Myles Chesterbrook told him to get us all out of here immediately."

"I was so caught up in the moment of the two of us coming together that I completely forgot about it. You guys notice the full moon with the pink glow?"

Everyone looked up and then back to Patrick in acknowledgement. "He told me that was called a 'Supermoon' and during this time the dead are at their strongest and can walk among us. He also told me that some of them are not happy."

"And you believe this dude?" Michael asked.

"Well, I'm pretty sure since I've just had a conversation with a man that's been dead for over twenty years!" Patrick responded, pointing again at the headstone. "So, yeah. I kinda believe him."

"Jerome?" Cassie asked, looking up at him with almost pleading eyes.

"I never wanted to come to this thing anyway. I only came so that I could use the opportunity to try and make things right with Patrick. Since I was able to do that and he's ready to leave, I have no issue with taking off. The only problem is getting Belinda and Derrick to come with us. They were actually looking forward to tonight."

"Don't you worry about them," Michael said. "I'll make sure they get home."

Cassie then turned to him and asked, "You want to stay?"

Smiling, Michael said, "I ain't afraid of no ghosts! But, if you want to leave with your friends, I won't hold it against you."

Cassie seemed hesitant, looking to Jerome and Patrick and then back to Michael before saying, "No, no I'll stay."

"Cassie," Patrick said, reaching out towards her. "Are you sure? I'm not fucking around here. I'm really scared, and I think you should be too!"

Almost defiantly, she wrapped her arms around Michael's waist and said, "Yes. Yes, I'm sure. Now you two go ahead and get out of here. Don't even bother to try and say goodbye to Belinda and Derrick. You know she'll throw a hissy-fit and a half and try to guilt you two into staying. So, avoid the drama and just go. I'll catch up with you tomorrow, ok?"

"Well," Jerome said, as he once again took Patrick's hand, "Only if you're sure."

"Don't worry fellas. I'll take good care of your girl," Michael said as he kissed Cassie on the forehead.

Jerome and Patrick then gave a quick nod to the pair and headed back down the path towards the entrance without looking back.

Cassie and Michael headed back towards the drink table and walked past an obviously drunk guy relieving himself against a headstone. They decided to stick with champagne and had just finished refilling their cups when the music abruptly stopped.

It was then that they noticed Jackie motioning for everyone to gather around her, so with drinks in hand they moved forward. Belinda and Derrick quickly joined them. Derrick asked, "Do you know what's about to happen?"

Michael responded, "I have no clue."

Looking around, Belinda asked, "Where are Jerome and Patrick? Did they ever get back?"

Cassie whispered in her ear, "Girl, you missed a lot! They did come back, but they had to leave. I'll fill you in on all the deets later. For now, let's hear what Ms. Diva has to say."

It was about that time that the group noticed that candles were being lit all around them.

Jackie held up her now nearly empty bottle and addressed the group, "Thank you friends for coming out to help me celebrate my birthday. You'll never know how much it means to me."

She then gestured to the surroundings as she continued, "I know the setting is a little unorthodox..."

Daniel quickly lost interest in what Jackie was saying. Like a moth to a flame, he was drawn to the girl he'd been eying earlier. She had long, flowing blonde locks styled with bouncy, wavy curls. He was mesmerized by her emerald-green eyes and full lips. The dress she was wearing was paper thin, possibly silk and stopped mid-thigh. The color was a shiny and bright orange the color of flame.

Looking directly at him and smiling sweetly, she motioned for him to follow her as she walked away from the gathering.

Grinning like a Cheshire Cat, he quickly obliged and followed her away from the party. She stopped briefly at a mausoleum, turned around to ensure he was following her and went inside.

Upon arriving at the entrance, Daniel did a quick look around to see if anyone noticed him before entering and closing the door behind him.

Allowing his eyes time to adjust, he noticed an abundance of lit candles and a few blankets on the ground in the middle of the room with the blonde standing in the center of them.

Upon locking eyes once more with Daniel, she slowly undressed, allowing her dress to fall to the floor revealing that she was not wearing any undergarments.

Needing no more encouragement, Daniel quickly undressed and joined the now naked girl on the blankets. Without saying a word, she grabbed his face and kissed him passionately. After a minute, she put both of her hands on his shoulders and applied the slightest pressure, guiding him to his knees. She then gently pushed his face between her legs and he eagerly and happily obliged.

After a moment of moaning in pleasure, she pushed Daniel onto his back and was happy to see that he was more than ready. She mounted him hungrily and began riding him with earnest. "My name's Emily," she said panting. "What's yours?"

"Daniel," he responded happily.

Meanwhile, Jackie was continuing with her speech, "You know, I've heard the rumblings and rumors that I think I'm a witch or voodoo priestess." As she mentioned 'voodoo priestess' she looked directly at Cassie, which caused the gossip to shiver involuntarily as Belinda gently nudged her.

"The truth of the matter is," Jackie continued, "I'm so much more. I come from a long line of immortals and I'm one of only a handful of necromancers."

Most of the people in the group began to murmur among themselves and there were even some audible nervous giggles as Belinda and Cassie exchanged puzzled looks.

"Yo! What the fuck is this crazy bitch on?" Derrick asked.

"I can assure you Derrick," Jackie said as she now focused her attention on him. "I am far from crazy. Tonight, I am not really celebrating my twenty-fifth. This evening actually marks one thousand years that I've walked this earth and I've brought along my real friends to mark the occasion. They've just been dying to meet you!"

Right at that moment, back inside the mausoleum, Daniel was on the verge of climaxing. Just as he closed his eyes, he felt something wiggly and wet hit his face. He opened his eyes again and screamed as maggots dripped from the now decaying flesh of Emily's face. The once beautiful woman now presented as skeletal, with strips of flesh hanging from her frame and wispy strands of blonde hair sticking out of her skull.

A horrified Daniel tried to wriggle free and throw Emily off of him, but she was too strong and had a firm grip on him in more ways than one. She tightened her grip around his private parts and said, "What's the matter lover? I just wanted to make you feel good!"

Daniel screamed even louder as Emily continued to ride him. Maggots were now dropping into his mouth which he tried desperately to spit out. Feeling helpless and now crying, he gave up struggling and went rigidly still.

"Daniel! Don't tell me you're done already! I was hoping you would last a little longer, but you've already gone limp on me! Oh, well. For the record I really did have fun but now I best be getting back to the party. Before I go though, there's one more thing I'm going to need from you."

An exhausted and emotionally drained Daniel forced himself to look into the now ugly visage of Emily. Without uttering a sound his expression said it all; What else can I possibly give you?

Emily threw her head back and let out a sickeningly loud cackle. "Oh, Daniel," she finally said, "You really are adorable. Now, I can't go back out there looking like this. What I need from you is your essence. Your life force will restore me to how I'm supposed to look."

At this point Daniel began to struggle again even harder than before. Because he had fooled Emily into thinking he had given up, he caught her off guard and was able to free himself. Once he was on his feet, he didn't even bother to grab his clothes. He threw the door open to the mausoleum and ran butt-naked towards the scene of the party.

The atmosphere at the party erupted into chaos as miscellaneous people dropped the façade, simultaneously revealing their true gruesome natures. Feeling something slimy in her hand, Cassie released her grip on Michael's and took a closer look at her hand while rolling her fingers together to figure out what it was that she was feeling.

Puzzled, she observed the viscous green substance and looked to Michael for answers. That's when her eyes opened wide in horror as she let out a blood-curdling scream. His flesh appeared rotted and decayed, with one eye dangling from the socket and resting on his cheek. The flesh of his lips was gone revealing nothing but teeth.

"Aww, don't be like that baby!" He said, "I thought we had a good thing going!" He then grabbed Cassie by both of her arms, pulled her in close and opened his mouth wide. She began shaking violently and uncontrollably as Michael 'fed' off of her life force. Her eyes rolled to the back of her head as her body began to rapidly deteriorate.

In less than thirty seconds, the only thing left of her were her clothes, which drifted listlessly to the ground as Michael's body was fully restored. "Cassie!" Belinda screamed as Derrick grabbed her hand and told her to run.

This scene repeated itself as various people were accosted and drained of their very being, disappearing into nothingness. Jackie, still atop her tree-stump perch watched the proceedings with drunken delight and laughed manically as the screams of the partygoers reached a deafening crescendo.

The screams grew so loud in fact, that Jerome and Patrick stopped dead in their tracks just as they were reaching the exit of the cemetery. "Did you hear that?" Patrick asked, grabbing Jerome's arm.

"I did," Jerome said. "Maybe we should go back?"

Patrick nodded and the two turned around to go back and try to retrieve their friends but standing in their path was Myles Chesterbrook.

"What the...?" A startled Jerome said.

"Wait! You... you can see him?" Patrick asked.

"What kind of question is that?" Jerome asked. "Of course, I can see him. He's standing right there in front of us!"

"Jerome, this is the man I was telling you about earlier. This is Myles Chesterbrook!"

Jerome looked back and forth from Patrick to Myles. He was beside himself and was having a hard time processing.

Myles took a tentative step forward and said, "Son, your friend Patrick is telling the truth. My name is Myles Chesterbrook and I was murdered in the summer of ninety-eight."

"I don't understand," Jerome said. "If that's true, how can I be having a conversation with you right now?"

"You know how son. You and Patrick are out of time. You have to leave now. Once you cross the threshold and are back onto the sidewalk outside of the entrance, you'll be safe, but you must hurry."

"But our friends! They're in trouble!"

"I'm afraid it's too late for them. Your friends are already dead."

"No!" Jerome said defiantly. "I don't accept that. We have to at least try!"

Frustrated that Jerome was not understanding the sense of urgency and seriousness of the situation at hand, Myles was no longer able to maintain his handsome image. Now angry, his true visage emerged, startling both Patrick and Jerome.

"I said you're out of time!" he bellowed. He stomped forward planting his right foot as he thrust out his arms hitting both Jerome and Patrick in the chest with the palms of his hands, propelling them backwards.

The pair were hit with enough force that they were knocked off of their feet and landed with a thud on their backs outside of the entrance of the cemetery. Upon hitting the ground, they both succumbed to unconsciousness.

Patrick was suddenly awakened by the sting of being slapped. Slowly, he opened his eyes to see Derrick kneeling over him with a relieved but awkward smile on his face. "Thank GOD you're alive!" Derrick said as he stood up, while pulling Patrick to his feet.

"What happened?" Patrick asked, dazed and confused.

"Yo! You won't believe the crazy shit that went down!" Derrick said.

"Cassie's dead!" screamed Belinda, who was standing behind Patrick which caused him to spin around to face her.

"What? Where's Jerome? He was with me when..."

"I'm right here!" Jerome said as he massaged the back of his head. "I feel like I've been hit by a Mack truck!"

Patrick ran to him and held him tight. "Thank GOD you're okay!"

Derrick and Belinda exchanged puzzled looks. "Um," Derrick began, "We're okay too, thanks for asking!"

"No, we are not okay!" Belinda screamed. "Cassie is dead! Does anyone give a fuck about that?"

Patrick broke from his embrace with Jerome and walked over to hug Belinda. "What happened?"

Belinda began shaking and uncontrollably crying in Patrick's arms, unable to respond.

"It's hard to describe man," Derrick said. That dude Michael that she was with?"

"Yeah?" Jerome said, walking closer to the group.

"He turned into some kind of fucking zombie! He grabbed Cassie, opened his mouth wide and she just, she just disappeared! Man, there was nothing left of her but her clothes! It was like a matter of seconds, and she was gone!"

"Oh my GOD!" Patrick screamed, looking past the group.

Belinda stopped crying and broke free from Patrick's arms as she and the rest of the group watched a naked and stumbling Daniel emerge from the cemetery. He collapsed just a few feet away from them as the sun began to rise on the horizon.

Derrick was the first to reach him. He removed his jacket and wrapped it around Daniel's waist. Daniel mumbled something inaudible which caused Jerome to lean in closer and say, "What was that, Bro? We couldn't hear you!"

Daniel, clearly exhausted, swallowed hard and loudly repeated, "Everybody's dead. They're all dead!"

Everyone in the group exchanged nervous glances before Patrick said, "Maybe we need to call the police!"

"And tell them what, exactly?" Belinda said, having already moved on from grief to anger. "Tell them that this psycho bitch we thought was our friend is actually an immortal necromancer?"

"Wait, what?" Patrick asked, clearly confused.

"Oh, that's right," Belinda said. "You two left before the real fun began."

Derrick jumped in by saying, "We didn't take her seriously at first when she told everyone that she wasn't celebrating her twenty-fifth birthday, she was actually celebrating her one thousandth. She then said that she was also a necromancer and her real friends were along to help her celebrate. That's when everything went bat-shit crazy."

Jerome stood up and said, "I need to go back and see if there are any survivors."

"Are you fucking nuts?!" Derrick screamed. "I barely got Belinda and myself out of there and you saw for yourself Daniel stumbling out of there without his fucking clothes for Christ's sakes! There's not a damn thing that you can do now!"

Patrick grabbed Jerome gently by the arm and said, "And let's not forget Myles Chesterbrook. You have to admit you thought I was a little bit nuts until you actually met him for yourself. Can we please just get the hell out of here before something else happens?"

Reluctantly, Jerome agreed and helped Derrick get Daniel to his feet. The group then made their way to Jerome's car, unaware they were being watched.

Three months later, it's a hot, sweltering evening at NE Eleventh Street in Miami Beach, Florida. The place, the flavor of the month dance bar known as Club Sultry. A lone, petite woman with shoulder length burnt orange locks slinks up to the bar to order a drink. Before she could get the bartenders' attention though, a dark-skinned, handsome stranger sidled up to her and said, "The names Jared beautiful. Would you mind if I got you a drink? I promise, no strings attached but I would like to try and get to know you."

Smiling sweetly, the woman responded, "Why thank you, Jared. I wouldn't mind at all. My name is Jackie and I have feeling that we are going to become the best of friends."

Blood Demon

It was one-thirty in the morning on this rain-drenched evening as paramedics burst through the emergency room doors of Kennedy Hospital. The female patient they were carrying on the gurney was covered in blood from head to toe. She lay motionless and with no expression. Her eyes were wide open and unblinking.

"Take her to Triage Three," Nurse Jenkins ordered while motioning for Dr. Blake and Orderly Parker to join them. Parker and the paramedics gathered around Dr. Blake as he said, "Okay, on my count, one, two... three!"

After transferring the patient to the bed, Dr. Blake said, "Okay, what have we got here?"

The paramedic known as Johnny spoke up, "As far as we can tell, the blood is not hers. There are no visible marks on her. Unfortunately, she doesn't have any ID on her either. We picked her up wandering the streets like this in Old City at Fourth and Chestnut. One of the restaurant owners in the area called 911. We haven't been able to get a single word out of her."

"The police are right behind us," April, the other paramedic added. "They want to question her."

"Well, we'll have to get her to speak first," Dr. Blake said as he continued his preliminary examination. He shined a penlight into her eyes to examine her pupils. "Hmm, she's dilated and has obviously experienced some sort of trauma."

He turned the light off and turned to face the rest of the room. "Well," he began addressing the paramedics. "I agree with you guys, there's no obvious physical signs of injury. You've done your part, you're free to go."

Both paramedics nodded and left without saying another word. Dr. Blake then addressed Nurse Jenkins. "Can you please page Dr. Miller? I believe she's on call tonight and this is more her area of expertise."

"Right away doctor." She quickly left the room.

Dr. Blake then turned to Parker the Orderly. "Just as a precaution, would you help me restrain her?"

"Sure thing doc!"

When that was completed, the two left the room and returned to the ER where a pair of detectives were waiting. Dr. Blake waived Parker off as he greeted them. "Good evening, detectives...?"

The taller of the two, dark-skinned and bald flashed his badge and said, "Good evening doctor. I'm Detective Williams and this is my partner, Detective Schuller. What can you tell us about the patient?"

"Not much I'm afraid. She's obviously traumatized about something, but she has no apparent physical injuries. She's covered in blood that isn't hers and she's been unresponsive."

It was at that exact moment that a blood-curdling scream emitted from the room where Jane Doe was being restrained. All available personnel within earshot ran towards the room.

Thrashing about and screaming at the top of her lungs, she pleaded, "It's gonna kill me! Don't let it get me! It took all my friends! Please help me! Please!"

"Nurse Jenkins!" Dr. Blake yelled, "Get me the B-52, stat!"

"B-52?" Detective Williams asked as Nurse Jenkins quickly placed a needle into the waiting doctor's hand.

Dr. Blake snatched the cap off the needle with his teeth and quickly administered the sedative to Jane Doe, who almost immediately calmed down and slumped back down onto the bed, her breathing returning to a normal rhythm.

The doctor disposed of the now empty needle and responded to the detective. "In short, B-52 is just a combination of Benadryl, Haloperidol and Lorazepam. I think you may be able to get a few answered questions out of her now, but you've got about twenty minutes before she'll be out for the count until morning.

"Thank you doctor."

Once the room was cleared of all medical personnel, Detective Williams pulled a chair up to the bed and sat down while Schuller remained standing just behind him.

"Hello, can you hear me? My name is Detective Williams. What's your name?"

Slowly, she turned her head to face him and said, "Cynthia. My name is Cynthia Pratt."

"Okay, Cynthia. Can you tell us what happened? You were found wandering the streets. Where were you?" Where did you come from?"

Before Cynthia could respond, Dr. Miller entered the room, accompanied by Dr. Blake. An attractive, middle-aged woman with salt and pepper hair, she was wearing tortoise shell Ottoto Bellona glasses. If it weren't for the white lab coat, she would resemble a sexy librarian. "Can't you see you're overwhelming her with these back-to-back questions?" she asked. She was not pleased in the least with the detective.

With both hands on her hips, she gave a stern look to both of the lawmen and stated. You get one question and one question only. Then, I'm afraid I'm going to have to ask you both to leave.

Detective Williams stood up quickly and said, "Dr., we have a possible homicide on our hands. Multiple, from the looks of things," he said motioning to a bloodied Cynthia. She has the answers we need to get this thing resolved as quickly as possible."

"Detective, I respect that you have a job to do but my first obligation is to my patient. This girl has obviously been traumatized and she needs to be treated mentally as well as physically. Bombarding her with questions right away is impeding any progress that we could make this evening. Ask your one question, allow me to do my job and you can come back in the morning to question her after she's been stabilized."

Detective Williams swallowed hard as he contemplated his next move. He found validity in what the doctor was saying, so he silently nodded an acknowledgement to her. He took out a pad and pen and turned to Cynthia and asked, "Can you give us the address of where you and your friends were tonight?"

A few minutes later, Williams and Schuller arrived at the one hundred block of North Bread Street in Old City, Philadelphia. It appeared to be a gated community but there were already two cop cars on the scene with flashing lights. One uniformed officer barely made it outside of the open gate before he puked all over the sidewalk.

Another officer quickly followed, accompanied by one of the residents. They walked up to Williams and Schuller. Williams, who recognized the officer spoke first, "Lenny. What do we have going on here?"

With a grim, and solemn look on his face, the officer said, "Detectives, this is Mr. Simms, a resident here. He's the one who called it in."

"I don't know much," the man said. "My wife and I were asleep when we heard all kinds of screaming. Of course, we were startled awake, so I got out of bed to investigate. The noises appeared to be coming from Unit E3 but the closer I got," Mr. Simms stopped briefly to shut his eyes and nod his head from side to side. He had come to the realization that this was one experience he would not be able to forget for quite some time. "I'm sorry," he said. "The noises I heard were indescribable, unlike anything I've ever heard in my life."

"Did you knock or attempt to enter?" Schuller asked.

"Hell no! Amongst all the screaming, I heard what sounded like bones snapping and this wet, poppy sound." Mr. Simms paused for a minute, as he massaged his temples. "I'm sorry," he said. "I just don't know how else to describe it. Anyway, I ran back to my place and called 911."

"Alright, thank you Mr. Simms," Officer Lenny said. "Officer Rush over there will take your statement, and we'll let you get back to your wife and home."

"Thank you." The man went over to the other cop as instructed.

Lenny returned his attention to the detectives and said, "Okay, follow me and I'll take you to the scene. Believe me when I say you have never seen anything like this in your life."

Williams and Schuller exchanged glances, then followed along silently. They entered the building and went up to the top floor. In the hallway, there were people milling about and everyone was wearing protective gear from head to toe. There was an odd smell emanating from Unit 3E. Officer Lenny instructed the detectives to put the gear and booties on and gave each of them a mask to put on.

"You're going to need this," he instructed as he stood aside.

"What?" Williams asked, "You're not coming in?"

"Oh, no!" Lenny said emphatically. "Once was more than enough! "I'll be here when you're done in case you need me for anything else."

Once again, Williams and Schuller exchanged glances before entering the home. The lights were on, illuminating the interior while the professionals were milling about dusting for fingerprints and taking photos, taking notes, etc. The first thing that the detectives noticed, however, was the amount of blood at the crime scene. It was literally everywhere. So much so, that there was no way to avoid stepping in it. Blood was even dripping from the ceiling and the walls.

"Oh, my GOD!" Schuller said. "What the hell happened here?"

Once they got over the shock of seeing so much blood, their eyes were then able to focus on the massacre itself. Body parts were strewn all over the place. Torsos, heads, arms, legs, organs, intestines, bodily fluids and worse. The scene repeated itself throughout the two thousand, five hundred square-foot residence.

The detectives gingerly made their way down to the lower level of the bi-level residence descending the wide, curved staircase. Upon reaching the ground floor, it was more of the same, blood, body parts and more blood.

The pair split and Williams was about to enter one of the guest rooms when Schuller called out for him to join him outside of the master bedroom. "What's up?" Williams asked as he hurried to his partner's side.

"Look," Schuller said pointing to the floor by the entrance. "Is it me or is that..."

"Salt," Williams said as he kneeled to touch the substance with his gloved hand. There was a line of it at the base of the bedroom door.

Confused, Schuller said, "What in the world...?"

Williams stood up, shrugged, and tried the door handle. The knob turned easily, so he turned to Schuller and said, it's not locked. Let's check it out."

Williams opened the door fully as they slowly entered the room. The spacious bedroom was spotless, not a drop of blood anywhere to be seen. They checked the walk-in closet, the bathroom ensuite with dual vanities, separate shower, and tub.

There was a wide, floor-length mirror on the wall near the entrance to the bathroom. At the base of it was another line of salt. Upon spotting it, Williams walked over to it and began feeling around the outer edges of the mirror.

"What are you doing?" Schuller asked.

"If my hunch is right," Williams started. Finding what he was looking for, he hit a switch and pulled the large mirror forward to reveal a panic room.

"Get the fuck out of here!" Schuller exclaimed. "How did you...?" He was cut off before he could finish his thought.

A wall monitor came to life and the face of a bespectacled, terrified young man filled the screen. "Hello? Who's out there?"

Williams pulled his badge and held it up to the monitor. "My name is Detective Williams and I'm standing out here with my partner, Detective Schuller, and you are?"

"Theodore Thompson but everyone just calls me Ted."

"Well, Ted. Can you please come out and talk to us? Tell us what happened here?"

"Everyone's dead, aren't they?"

"I'm afraid so Ted."

"Okay, stand back please. I'm going to come out."

Williams took a step back and as a precaution, he and Schuller pulled their weapons but pointed them towards the floor.

As the door to the panic room swung out, Ted slowly emerged, clutching a thick, leather-bound book. Upon seeing the guns, he immediately threw his hands up and said, "I swear to you I'm not armed!"

Williams gave a nod to Schuller and they both quickly holstered their weapons. "Okay, Ted. We didn't mean to startle you, but we've just walked through a massacre.

Ted suddenly dropped to his knees and began sobbing. "It's all my fault! I didn't think it was real. Nobody did. It was supposed to just be a stupid party game."

Williams again gave a look to Schuller. They went to either side of Ted and helped him to his feet. They guided him to the foot of his bed and sat him down. There were two chairs in the room, so they each grabbed one and took a seat in front of him.

Schuller pulled out a pad and pen and said, "Okay Ted, can you walk us through the events of the day? Start by telling us what you have there. You're clutching that book as if it's something important."

Ted inhaled deeply, wiped his eyes and finger-combed his curly brown hair back out of his face. He looked at the detectives and said, "I'll tell you everything that I know but you're not going to believe me. You may even think that I'm crazy."

Williams leaned back, crossed his legs, and said, "Try us."

Ted took another deep breath and began his tale. "I closed on this place about a month ago. A handful of my friends and coworkers helped me put together a housewarming party. That's what tonight was supposed to be about. Anyway, about a week ago I was walking along the three hundred block of South Street and spotted this old bookstore called the Talisman. Out of curiosity I went inside.

It was a lot bigger than it looks from the outside and they carry more than books. I saw Tarot Cards, candles, crystals, incense, sage, all kinds of interesting stuff. There was a section dedicated to Demonology, so for shits and giggles I browsed over the books and this one caught my eye."

Ted held up the book and handed it to Detective Williams. The leather embossed book had a red stone in the center of what looked like an eye on the cover. "Go ahead and open it," Ted instructed.

Williams undid the clasp and opened the book to the first page. He involuntarily gasped at the incredibly detailed image that was rendered in color. It resembled a cross between big boot and the devil. The body appeared large and was covered in shaggy brown fur. The face was the color of crimson and the jade green eyes appeared to glow. Long, tan horns protruded from the skull on either side of the head above pointy ears and the mouth was open, showcasing long pointy fangs. The feet were cloven hoofs, but the hands sported long, razor-like claws.

Beneath the image was the caption in big, bold letters, **'DEAMHAN oio FUIL'**. Williams handed the book to Schuller and said to Ted, "Are you trying to tell us that this is what killed everyone here this evening? What is that caption underneath?"

"Jesus!" Schuller exclaimed before quickly handing the book back to Ted.

"I told you that you wouldn't believe me. I didn't believe it was real either. The rest of the book is in a combination of English and Gaelic. Irish Gaelic to be specific. ***Deamhan oio Fuil*** translates to Demon of Blood."

"Alright," Williams said. "You obviously purchased the book and brought it home. Fast forward to today and the party."

"Okay. Well, everyone who was invited showed up. We had plenty of food and refreshments and we were all having a great time. At some point I was called into my living room and saw that one of my guests was holding the book in her hands. I had forgotten about it after placing it on my coffee table."

"And what is the name of the guest that was holding the book?" Schuller asked as he took notes.

Ted massaged the back of his neck before answering. "It's someone I was trying to work up the nerve to ask out. Her name is… was Cindy."

Schuller stopped writing and looked at Williams. He was about to say something when Williams quickly and silently nodded no. Signaling his partner to keep quiet about the sedated woman at the hospital for now.

"Go on," Williams said.

"Well, Cindy found this passage in the book." Ted opened the book and flipped the pages to the section he was looking for. Again, he turned the book around and handed it to Williams.

"The Summoning?" Williams read aloud the title of the passage before handing the book back.

"Yes. Cindy wanted to ask me if it would be okay to try it, to read the passage out loud. I said sure, why not? So, we gathered about six or eight of us, I can't remember the exact number at this time, but we sat on the floor in a circle. We enclosed ourselves in a circle of salt, lit a candle in the center of the circle and Cindy read the passage out loud. When she was done, a breeze blew out the candle. Someone screamed and then we all laughed, figuring someone blew the candle out deliberately for effect.

We all stood up and Cindy handed me the book. Everyone headed towards the kitchen for drinks, and I was about to put the book back on the table when the real screaming started. I turned around to see what the fuss was about and that's when I saw it. It looked exactly like this drawing in the book, but it had to have been at least seven feet tall.

It was ripping through people as if they were paper dolls. I couldn't believe my eyes and I didn't know what to do. I grabbed the salt and the book, and I ran to the panic room and tried to protect myself with more salt. Once inside I went through the book looking for a banishment spell or a containment spell. Something, anything to keep that thing from getting out. It must have worked too if you both are able to sit and calmly listen to me without anything happening and everyone from the party is dead."

Again, Williams and Schuller exchanged looks, this time Ted realized something was up. "Okay, what is going on? You don't seriously think I'm capable of killing all those people in that manner, do you? Damn, it! I knew you wouldn't believe me."

"Ted, try and calm down," Williams said. "With the amount of blood that's been shed, there's no way that you would be able to present yourself as spotless as you are. We know you didn't do it. It's just that I'm having a hard time believing this was the work of some demon."

"Did your partygoers partake in any recreational drugs by chance?" Schuller asked.

"That's not something that I condone or indulge in myself. So, I can confidently say no. I would not knowingly allow that to happen in my home. Besides, you both have to admit that no human is capable of causing this amount of destruction with their bare hands."

"Maybe," Williams said. "There's one more thing we need to discuss."

"What's that?"

Williams looked at Schuller and nodded, giving him the go ahead.

Schuller closed his notepad and said, "You said Cindy found the book and read the passage, correct?"

"Yes, that's right."

"Her name wouldn't be Cynthia Pratt by any chance, would it?"

"OMG! Yes! That's her name! How do you..."

"She's alive, Ted." Williams said. She was admitted to Kennedy Hospital not too long ago. She was found wandering the streets covered in blood."

"No! No, no, no, no!" Ted exclaimed as he frantically flipped through the pages of the book again.

"Schuller said, "What's the problem? I thought you liked this girl. Aren't you happy she's alive?"

Finding the page he was looking for, Ted said, "You're still not grasping the seriousness of what I've been trying to tell you." He handed the book to Schuller and pointed to a passage. "Read that out loud so Detective Williams can hear you."

Sighing heavily, Schuller accepted the book and read the following out loud as instructed, "Be warned, summoning the Demon of Blood means to surrender your body and soul completely as he cannot be called to return to hell for forty days. The summoner is doomed to take his place in hell and upon his return will be forced to remain at his side in damnation for all eternity."

Without warning, Ted made a dash for the panic room, but Williams was anticipating such a move and tackled him before he could reach the threshold. He swiftly put his handcuffs on him and stood Ted up who began protesting loudly.

"I didn't want to do this to you, but you can't stay here even if we wanted you to. This is now a crime scene."

Ted began to shake and cry as he said, "I thought I had defeated that thing. The only way he was able to leave was by possessing Cindy. Don't you see? That's why he kept her alive."

Williams exchanged glances with Schuller again and said, "If I lead you out of here in handcuffs everyone will assume that you are our prime suspect. Do you want that?"

Ted silently nodded his head no.

"Okay then. We'll take you wherever you like but you need to come with us. If I remove these cuffs, do you promise to behave and not try to bolt again?"

A silent nod of yes.

Williams removed the cuffs and Schuller handed the man back his book. The three then made their way up and out of the bloodied residence. Patiently waiting in the hallway, was Officer Lenny as he had promised.

He walked up to the three and said, "Holy shit! You found a survivor! Wait! Is he the...?"

"No Lenny," Williams said. We believe he is innocent but obviously he can't stay here. Walk with us?"

"Yeah! Yeah, sure."

Meanwhile, back in the hospital… in a dark and quiet room Cynthia was sleeping soundly when Orderly Parker sneaked in and closed the door behind him. He walked over to the bed and gently caressed the sleeping woman's lips.

After touching himself briefly, he turned Cynthia's head to face him and slightly opened her mouth. He dropped his pants and as he inched closer to her face, her eyes suddenly opened wide and glowed and intense bright green. Startled, Parker jumped backwards, tripped, and fell squarely on his ass with a loud thump.

Still strapped to the bed, Cynthia sat upright and swung her feet over the bed, snapping her restraints with ease. Never taking her glowing eyes off the orderly, she stood up and walked slowly towards him. He desperately tried to pull his pants back up as he backed up away from her. It wasn't long before he hit the wall though and panic began to seep into the core of his being.

"Look, I don't know what you think was happening, but…" he stopped mid-sentence. Cynthia stopped walking and stood completely still for a second. The glow momentarily left her eyes and she reached out a hand to Parker in an almost pleading gesture.

Confused, Parker reached out for her hand in return but in an instant, he was bathed in blood as Cynthia's body seemed to explode and standing in her place was a seven-foot, hairy, red-face demon. The glowing green eyes returned and seemed to burn directly into his soul. Parker barely had time to scream before the demon removed his head from his body and tossed it aside.

It was at this precise moment that Dr. Miller came to check on her patient. She opened the door, saw the carnage and the demon standing in the middle of the room and let out a blood-curdling scream. Like a sprinter in the Olympics, she spun on her heels and made a mad dash for the Nurse's Station, screaming for Nurse Jenkins to call the police.

Without hesitation, the nurse dialed nine-one-one. The responder barely had time to acknowledge the call when all he heard were screams and other sickening sounds.

After loading Ted into the back of their vehicle, Detectives Williams and Schuller, along with Officer Lenny heard the dispatcher call for all available units to respond to a distress call at Kennedy Hospital. They all jumped into their respective vehicles and with sirens blaring and lights flashing, raced to the hospital.

When they arrived, there were several other emergency responders already on the scene. As Williams and Schuller prepared to exit, Ted went into full on freak out mode. "What are you doing?" he yelled. "Have you not heard a single word that I've said? You don't stand a chance against that thing!"

Williams responded, "Even if everything that you told us is true, I still have a job to do. There are people in there that need my help. I cannot turn my back on them. If you truly believe this thing, this demon is real, cause I've gotta be honest with you, I don't, look through that book of yours and find a way to stop it once and for all."

That notion had the desired effect and seemed to calm Ted down. It gave him a sense of purpose. He began flipping through the book in earnest, searching for a miracle. Satisfied, Williams motioned for Schuller and Officer Lenny to proceed. They rushed into the entrance of the hospital and stopped almost immediately in their tracks.

Once inside they immediately felt a sense of de ja vu. They walked into a horrific all to familiar scene. Officer Lenny began to sweat profusely. There was blood and body parts everywhere. Officer Lenny spun around to face Williams and Schuller. "Is what that guy in your car said for real? This is the work of some fucking demon?"

Before either detective could respond, they all heard a low guttural sound that grew increasingly louder. When Williams and Schuller suddenly pulled their guns and pointed over his head, Officer Lenny immediately pissed himself, but he forced himself to turn around to face what was obviously behind him.

Matted in blood and viscera, the demon stood before the trio of lawmen holding the lifeless body of Dr. Blake. After snapping the body in half as if it were a dry branch and tossing it aside, it lunged for Officer Lenny. That's when Williams and Schuller opened fire causing the demon to take a few steps backwards.

Ted looked up briefly from the book upon hearing the gunshots and cursed before returning his attention to finding something, anything that could help him. He continued furiously flipping through the pages until he spotted what he was looking for.

"Shit!" he cursed again after quickly reading the banishment spell. "I don't have anything with me that I would need to effectively get rid of this thing." He was about to give up hope when he remembered what he attempted to do the first time. "No!" he said aloud to himself. "That would only be a temporary fix."

Frustrated, Ted closed the book and massaged his temples. Suddenly, he heard screaming coming from the hospital. "Fuck, it!" he said. "Doesn't look like I have much of a choice." He rifled through the book once more to the page he needed and immediately recited what he had much earlier in the evening back at his home.

Inside the hospital, Williams, Schuller, and Lenny had emptied their weapons and were out of ammunition. As Lenny was the closest to the demon, he was the first one he grabbed and lifted off the ground. The officer experienced pain like he had never experienced before, causing him to yell out.

Before any real damage could be done however, the demon froze. Looking past Officer Lenny, it locked eyes with Detective Williams for a second, and then it just vanished, leaving Lenny to fall to the ground in a heap.

Schuller rushed to the fallen officer's side and said, "What the fuck just happened? Where'd that thing go?"

"Who gives a shit?" Lenny said as he got to his feet. "Let's get the hell out of here before it comes back!"

Williams rushed to Lenny's side and helped Schuller escort him out of the hospital and back onto the street. Once Ted spotted them, he got out of the car to greet them. "What happened?" he asked.

"Everyone is dead. We're the only survivors and that's just barely so. Whatever you did worked."

"I told you all that thing was real. What do we do now?"

"We go back to the precinct." Williams said. "We'll regroup and figure out what to do next."

Officer Lenny was loaded into the back seat with Ted, while Schuller rode shotgun and Williams took the driver's seat. As soon as the engine started Ted said, "Wait a minute. I don't think I need to go down to the station with you all. I can just get a hotel room and hook back up with you guys in the morning."

"I'm sorry Ted but that's not going to work for me," Williams said as he electronically locked all the doors.

"Why not?" Schuller asked. He got rid of the damned thing. It's over."

Struggling with the door to get out, Ted said, "That's the problem. It's not over. I couldn't properly banish the demon because I don't have any of the required instruments or tools that I needed. Now let me out of this car dammit!"

At this point Williams started the vehicle and pulled away from the latest crime scene. A now drowsy Lenny said, "What's going on? What do you mean it's not over?"

Still fighting with the door even more frantically now, Ted responded, "The only thing I was able to do was bind it to that place, just like I did earlier this evening in my home."

"Wait a minute!" Schuller said. He turned in his seat to face Ted. "I think I know where you're going with this but none of us summoned that thing. Why can't it still be stuck there inside the hospital?"

Exasperated, Ted leaned back in his seat and said, "I don't know. I never claimed to be an expert on this shit! Did it lock eyes with any of you before it disappeared?"

"What? No, I don't think so."

"Ted. You're too smart for your own damned good!" Williams said. "For someone who claims to not know much, you seem to know an awful lot."

"Williams?" Schuller asked as he turned back around in his seat to face his partner. "What's wrong with your voice?"

Williams looked at his partner, smiled impossibly wide and sported razor-like teeth. His eyes now resembled green flames. The mere sight of him caused Schuller to throw himself back against the passenger side door and scream. The two men in the back seat soon joined in and they all frantically tried to escape.

The screams of the trapped men echoed as the car sped off into the night.

LOVER'S KISS

No sooner had Xander ordered a Manhattan from the sexy bartender did his phone go off. Answering it quickly, he said, "Mark, where are you guys? I just ordered a drink." Suddenly frowning, he said into his cell, "Aw man, that's too bad. I was looking forward to seeing you guys. No, of course I understand. We'll get together another time. Feel better, okay? Tell Jake I said hello. Alright, bye."

Disappointed, Xander set his phone down on the bar just as the bartender returned with his drink. With a slight smile, he paid for the cocktail and took a sip. Just then he felt a tap on his shoulder. He turned to see a tall handsome man with jet black hair and ice blue eyes. "Excuse me," the stranger began, "Is this seat taken?"

"No," Xander said. "Not at all. Have a seat."

Smiling, the stranger said, "Thank you."

The bartender came over and said, "What can I get you hon?"

"A glass of Merlot, please."

"Coming right up!"

Xander took another sip of his drink. The stranger reached out his hand and said, "Hi, my name is Sage."

Xander reciprocated the gesture and said, "Like the herb?"

With a slight chuckle, Sage said, "Yes, exactly. And your name?"

"Oh, sorry! My name is Xander." He was beside himself and a little caught off guard that this insanely beautiful man was striking up a conversation with him.

The bartender returned with the glass of wine and Sage handed him a credit card and said I'd like to open up a tab please and back up my new friend here with whatever he's drinking."

The bartender accepted the card, smiled, nodded, and walked away.

"You didn't have to do that," Xander said."

"No worries. Besides, if you don't mind me saying so, when I walked up you looked like you could use some cheering up."

"Oh, no. I'm fine. I was just disappointed. I was supposed to meet some friends of mine here tonight, but one of them is feeling a little under the weather, so they decided to stay in."

"Well, that's too bad. Their loss though, is my gain." Sage held up his glass and gestured for Xander to do the same.

Now blushing, Xander clinked his glass and thought to himself, "Is this guy seriously flirting with me?"

As time went on, Xander found himself feeling more and more relaxed, and just a little tipsy. Sage was easy to talk to and the direct eye contact and polite smiles soon graduated to soft caresses and hand holding. Before he knew it, they were kissing and making out.

Suddenly, someone shouted, "Get a room!" This caused the pair to take a breath and they both started laughing.

"You know," Sage said as gestured for the bartender. "Whoever that was has a point. Why don't we get out of here? Can I entice you to come back to my place?"

Xander thought about it for a second and said, "Yeah, okay. Let's do it. Where do you live?"

"A quick cab ride from here down Chestnut Street. About a block from Penn's Landing."

After Sage settled his tab, the pair made their way outside where it was now raining heavily. Luckily, they were able to hail a cab fairly quickly and arrived less than ten minutes later at Sage's home. Upon entering the foyer, Sage said, "Leave your shoes here and follow me."

Xander did as instructed and followed his host, all the while admiring the interior of the home. The two-story foyer boasted a beautiful modern art design crystal spiral chandelier. The s-shaped design with the cascading lights just added to the regality.

The furnishings were mahogany with royal blue crushed velvet and gold accents. There were high end lamps, artwork on the walls, and expensive rugs, among other things. The place just reeked of money. Xander was wondering just who this guy was when he had apparently reached his destination.

"Alright, let's get you out of these wet clothes." When Xander smiled mischievously, Sage smirked and said, "In due time mister. I have a robe for you to protect your modesty." He laid the silk robe over a chair and removed his clothes as well.

Xander couldn't help but stare and admire his hosts' physique. It was if he had been chiseled and sculpted from marble. He couldn't see an ounce of fat anywhere. He was simply, breathtaking. He was slightly disappointed when Sage put on a robe himself.

Once he was free of his wet clothes, Sage scooped them up and said, "I'll put these in the dryer for you. In the meantime, make yourself comfortable. Can I offer you a drink?"

"Um, yeah, sure!"

"What would you like? I have a full bar."

"Really? Well, why don't you surprise me."

"I can do that. I like your sense of adventure. I'll be back before you know it."

Xander smiled and took a seat on a plush, velvet round arm sofa, this one was gold with blue accent pillows. He practically sank into the comfortable piece of furniture and before he knew it, Sage was waking him up, holding the drink he had prepared for him.

"Oh, my GOD! I'm so sorry!" Xander said as he sat himself back up and received the drink. "I was so comfortable; I must have dozed off."

"No apologies necessary," Sage said as he sat beside Xander. "So, what do you think?"

"Hmm?"

"Of the drink. Do you like it?"

"It's delicious! What is it?"

"A gimlet. There are vodka gimlets, but I made this one with gin. Glad you like it."

Xander nodded and took another sip before setting the drink down on the end table.

Sage could sense that Xander was pondering something, so he asked, "What's on your mind?"

"Can I ask you something?"

"Anything!"

"Why me?"

"Pardon?"

"Don't get me wrong. You are a beautiful man. It appears to me that you could have your pick of anyone you wanted. I'm just not sure what I could bring to the table."

"Interesting…"

"Aw, man! I don't mean to sound presumptuous, it's just that…"

Sage gently placed a finger on Xander's mouth and said, "Shhh!!! Allow me to answer your question. First, don't sell yourself so short. It's true, I don't lack for most things, only the most important and that's companionship. I sense in you something that I can't quite put my finger on, but I know that I like it and I want more of it!" Sage stopped speaking when he saw Xander smiling with the return of a mischievous twinkle in his eye.

Xander climbed on top of him, wrapped his arms tightly around his neck and kissed him passionately. When he finally came up for air, he said, "Good answer! I like you too!"

Unable to control themselves any longer, the pair shed their robes and succumbed to the unbridled passion bubbling just beneath the surface.

They never even made it off the couch and when they were done, Sage cradled Xander who rubbed his chest, mumbled something, then promptly fell asleep.

Sage understood what Xander had said. He smiled and closed his eyes as well.

A few hours later, Xander woke up with a start, temporarily forgetting where he was. Candles were lit all around the room. He sat up and smiled, remembering how good Sage had made him feel. He looked around and wondered where his host was. He had a sudden urge to pee, so he left the room in search of a bathroom, never bothering to grab the silk robe he'd worn earlier.

He happened upon some heavy French doors and realized that there was no way there was a bathroom on the other side, but curiosity had a hold of him. He was about to open them when he was startled by the presence of a stranger who said, "Do you require assistance sir?"

Xander spun around to see a handsome and muscular, tall blonde man, standing there. He appeared to be in his forties dressed all in black. Tightfitting t-shirt, black jeans, belt, and loafers. Xander's heart plummeted to his stomach like a stone in the lake and then he suddenly remembered that he was naked. He quickly cupped his private parts in his hands out of sheer embarrassment.

"I'm so sorry," he began, "I didn't know anyone else was here. I was looking for a bathroom and I seem to have lost Sage as well."

"Don't worry. I'll take you to him, he's expecting you. But first, let's get you to the bathroom."

As the stranger began walking away, Xander followed and said, "Thank you. My name is Xander by the way."

The stranger turned briefly with a smile and carried on walking as he stated, "Nice to meet you, Xander. My name is Gabriel. I'm Mr. Sage's Assistant. I manage and maintain his properties." He then stopped walking and made a gesture towards a door. "Here we are Xander. I'll be out here when you're done and take you to Mr. Sage."

Still feeling awkward, Xander said, "Okay, thank you Gabriel," as he entered the bathroom and closed the door. His head spinning as he relieved himself, he felt slightly better that Gabriel didn't turn out to be Sage's boyfriend, but still he wondered, *Who is this guy? I mean, who has a personal assistant in their home at this time of the night?*

After washing and drying his hands, he was about to exit the bathroom when he paused, realizing that he was still naked. He then shook his head, remembering that Gabriel had already seen him in all his glory. He snatched the door open with resolve and was surprised and happy to see that Gabriel was holding open the robe that he'd been wearing earlier.

Thanking him profusely, he slipped the garment on and cinched it closed at the waist. Once more, he blindly followed Gabriel and was once again surprised to find himself back at the double doors he was about to enter thru earlier. Gabriel pulled them open and then stepped aside to allow Xander to enter the room.

The parlor room was dark and dimly lit, but the first thing that Xander noticed was the fact that positioned in the middle of the room were two large coffins. A chill went up his spine as he spun around to question Gabriel, who was already closing the doors.

Xander could hear Gabriel locking him inside the room, but he tried the doors nevertheless and shouted, "Hey! What's going on? Don't lock me in here! Let me out!"

"Calm yourself, Xander," a voice came from behind.

Xander spun around again and saw Sage sitting calmly in a chair off to the corner of the room. Xander took a few tentative steps toward him and said, "Sage? What's happening? Why did you bring me here?"

Sage took his time and stood up slowly. He knew that Xander was already freaking out, so as he eased his way closer to him, he said, "Is that really what you want to ask me?"

Xander combed his fingers through his hair and massaged the back of his neck before responding, "Yes! I mean, no! I have a million questions but why do you have coffins in here? What is this? What is it that you do?"

With a slight smile, Sage said, "I'm an antiquities dealer. The coffins are just for show. A symbolic gesture. I don't really need them."

"Need them for what?"

"I think you already suspect," Sage said. At this point he was standing directly in front of Xander. Gently, he brushed the back of his fingers against the side of Xander's face before moving behind him and holding him around the waist. Slowly, he opened Xander's robe and pressed up against him as he caressed the front him. First, he massaged his chest, taking great care with his nipples before moving lower to his now fully engaged manhood.

He began to slowly stroke him as he continued to speak, barely above a whisper in Xander's ear, "You asked me why I picked you when the truth of the matter is, you made quite the impression on me slightly over a year ago. We first met at a rooftop party, in Rittenhouse Square. Before our conversation could go anywhere, one of your inconsiderate friends pulled you away."

Completely aroused and breathless, Xander managed to say, "I'm... sorry... I don't... remember..."

"It's okay, sweetheart." Sage said. "I've kept tabs on you, and you deserve so much better than what you've been given. I can give that to you if you'll allow me."

Xander nodded his head yes, but Sage knew that what he was asking was not completely understood. Yet. He stopped pleasuring Xander long enough to remove his own robe, rub some lubricant on himself and he entered Xander from behind with blinding speed, taking care not to injure him in the process. Xander cried out. Not in pain, but in pure ecstasy.

The pair found their way to the chair that Sage had previously been sitting in and it was here that he sat down again. Xander placed a hand on each of Sage's shoulder's and proceeded to ride him as if they were in the Kentucky Derby. They both cried out, climaxing at the same time and Xander, a sweaty mess, collapsed on top of Sage.

With no effort, Sage stood up and carried Xander towards the doors which seemed to open instantly. He walked to his master bedroom and into the ensuite. Sage did not put Xander down until they were in the middle of a huge four-person shower with multiple rainfall shower heads. He turned the water on and said, "Let me know if it gets too hot for you."

Xander smiled and said, "I will."

As the pair soaped up, Sage said, "Do you remember what you said to me after we made love on the couch but before you fell asleep?"

Xander smiled and said, "I do, and I meant every word. I said that I could fall in love with you."

Sage said, "I hope you mean that because I'm already in love with you. I have been for quite some time; I just haven't been able to express or show it until now."

"Why did you wait so long?"

"I wanted to be sure you were ready. I'm still not sure but I just couldn't stand to be apart from you any longer."

Xander stopped moving and looked at Sage with conviction before stating, "I'm ready. You are right. My friends treat me like shit and often make me feel like an afterthought. You've made me feel things in just a few short hours that opened my eyes to what I've been missing my whole life. I'll say it again. I'm ready. I want to be with you."

"Have you accepted what I am? What you'll become? There's no going back."

"I'm committed. I'm giving you my full consent."

"Excellent!" Sage said as he stepped closer to his intended. His ice-blue eyes glowed with an intensity of miniature suns as he opened his mouth to release a pair of fangs. Xander became rigidly still as Sage sank into the flesh of his neck and began to drink his life's blood.

Sage did not stop until Xander collapsed. He then carried him dripping wet into the master bedroom. Gabriel had laid out a pile of towels across the king-sized bed and it was here that Sage gently laid his intended down on. He then splayed his hands to release claw-like nails. He cut open a vein and poured the blood from his body into the open mouth of Xander.

He stood over him letting his blood drip for about thirty seconds. He then licked his wrist and the wound rapidly closed and healed in a matter of seconds. Gabriel helped Sage towel Xander dry, then carefully removed them while he slept. They then covered him up with a blanket up to his neck.

Sage bent down, kissed Xander on the lips and said, "Sleep well my beloved. When you reawaken, your new life will begin." He then stood up and put a hand on Xander's forehead and rubbed his hair backwards. He looked at Gabriel and said, "I trust that everything is ready?"

Gabriel smiled, handed Sage a robe and said, "Yes we are all set."

The pair then exited the bedroom and headed back to the parlor room with the two coffins. Sage opened one of them and Gabriel opened the other. Inside each of the coffins were Xander's friends, Mark and Jake, the couple that was supposed to meet him out for drinks earlier that evening. They were tightly bound and gagged, trying to scream and move.

"You lot have hurt my beloved for the last time," Sage said. "When he awakes, he'll be absolutely famished. I'm positive that you'll be dying to make it up to him!"

Sage laughed as he and Gabriel closed the coffin lids over the terrified occupants.

STRAWBERRY MANSION

It was a wet and chilly night in Philadelphia due to a torrential downpour that did not seem to be slowing down anytime soon. A patrol car came to an abrupt stop near the corner of Thirty-Third Street and Ridge Avenue.

Two uniformed officers exited their vehicle and made their way to a prisoner transport vehicle sitting idle at a traffic light. Both officers pulled their weapons and flashlights as one approached the driver's side and the other the passenger window. Upon peering inside the passenger window, Officer Hernandez immediately withdrew, shouting, "Ay Dios Mio!" as he threw up on the sidewalk.

Officer Jackson looked on in disbelief as he shown his light on his brutally murdered colleagues. Their throats were slashed, and they were also disemboweled, intestines in full display on the victims' laps. He also withdrew and moved quickly to the back of the van and opened the back to see that it was empty. Speaking rapidly into his shoulder walkie talkie, he said, "Dispatch, we've found Thomas and Zhang. They're both dead! Repeat, they are both dead! Send all available units to our location ASAP. Harold the Butcher is on the loose!"

Not too far away, a car came to an abrupt stop on Kelly Drive. "What the fuck, Jerry!" Keith yelled from the back seat. "Don't tell me this piece of shit died on you again! I knew we should have taken my car!"

"Calm down baby," his girlfriend Anna said. "You're just messing around aren't you, Jerry? Playing some kind of joke on us?"

Sighing heavily, Jerry laid his head on the steering wheel and said, "Sorry Anna. I wish I was, but the car just gave out on me." He tried to start it again, but the vehicle did not make a sound. It was dead.

In the passenger seat was Jerry's girlfriend Sabrina. "Well, can't we just call Triple A or something?" she asked.

"I don't have Triple A babe," Jerry said. "I'll try to call a tow truck, but we can't stay here. It's not safe."

"And where are we supposed to go genius?" Keith asked. "In case you haven't noticed, it's raining cats and dogs right now!"

Jerry turned around to face his friend. "Since when are you afraid of a little water? We can make our way over to Strawberry Mansion. It's not too far from here."

"Are you nuts? First, at this time of night that place will be sealed tighter than a drum. Second, we'll be drenched by the time we get there, and it's pitch black between here and there."

"Are you done with the excuses? It's not safe for us to stay here. You know some of these drivers don't pay attention to what they're doing. Someone could plow into us at any minute. The mansion has an overhang at the entrance, so we don't have to stand in the rain until help arrives. Now, you're free to chill here if you like but I'm going to take my chances at the mansion."

Jerry then turned back around in his seat and asked Sabrina to retrieve a flashlight from the glovebox. Everyone exited the car except for Keith.

"Come on Keith!" Anna said. "You know he's right. It's not safe for you to stay here!"

Frowning, Keith begrudgingly exited the car and took his girlfriend's hand.

Just as they made their way a few feet away from the car, they heard the screeching of tires and a loud horrendous crash. Everyone turned around quickly to see that someone had indeed plowed into Jerry's car with such force that it was most definitely totaled. The driver had obviously not been wearing a seat belt, as he was through the windshield, sprawled out against the crumpled hood of his car. Blood and glass were everywhere, with the obviously now deceased driver's eyes wide open and glazed over.

The girls screamed and the guys turned them away from the crash. "Don't look," Jerry yelled, as he tried to shield Sabrina from the horrific site.

Keith did the same with Anna and said, "There's nothing we can do for that poor soul now. Let's get the hell out of this rain and call for help."

In silence, the foursome made their way to Strawberry Mansion and stood at the entrance under the portico. Everyone was still pretty shaken up with what they had just witnessed, and the girls were starting to shiver from the whole ordeal.

For no reason, Keith decided to try the door and was shocked that it gave way. "Hey guys," he said. "This motherfucker is open! Let's go inside!"

"What?" Jerry asked. How?"

"Who cares! Come on. Let's get out of this weather!"

No one needed any more convincing, so they followed him inside and closed the door. The interior was pitch-black, so they all felt along the walls for a light switch. Sabrina turned on the flashlight she'd taken from the car and Anna pulled out her cell phone for an extra light source.

Just as Anna spotted a lamp, she also thought she saw a figure move in the shadows. She gasped and quickly turned on the lamp. There was nothing there.

Keith came up behind and gently touched her shoulders. "Hey, Babe. Are you okay?"

A shiver went up her spine causing her to involuntarily shake. She quickly collected herself and forced herself to smile as she turned to face her boyfriend. "I'm fine. It's just that I thought I saw someone before I turned the lamp on, but there's no one there."

"No worries, babe, Jerry and I will check this place from top to bottom."

Jerry came over and said, "Absolutely. Since the door was open, it makes sense that someone would be here. We probably scared whoever it is. We'll just explain that we mean no harm and tell them what happened to us tonight."

Sabrina came over to stand beside Jerry and kissed him gently on the lips before grabbing his face with both hands. "Nevertheless," she began, "I want you both to be careful. This place is creepy at night."

Anna turned around and gave Keith a kiss. She then said, "We'll call the police while you're ensuring our safety. Considering the circumstances, I don't think we'll get into any serious trouble."

"You do that Babe! I'll see you soon!"

The men then proceeded to search the ground floor. Keith suddenly stopped Jerry and said, "Look man, I owe you an apology. You saved my life back there. I'm sorry about giving you a hard time about the car."

"We're good, man. You know I love you."

"Yeah, but like a brother, right?"

Jerry laughed and said, "Yes, asshole! Like a brother."

Keith laughed as well and as the pair came across a room he felt around for a light switch. Upon finding one he flipped it and gave a slight whistle. "Hey, check out the piano and the harp! What room is this, you figure?"

"Probably the ballroom. Yeah, I think that's what this is."

"Pretty cool! Do you play?" Keith said as he sat down and struck a few keys.

"No. I was never musically inclined."

Keith got up and said, "Yeah, me neither."

They exited the room and cleared the rest of the downstairs before heading upstairs.

Jerry pulled out his phone to use as a light source and Keith did the same as they ascended the stairs to the second floor. "Hey," Jerry began, "Do you think Anna really saw something or was it her imagination playing tricks on her?"

"Who the hell knows man?" Keith said. "But I tell you what, she's got a damn good head on her shoulders, so if she says she saw something, better believe it. How else would you explain the front door being open?"

"Good point. Maybe we should have looked around for some weapons or something to protect ourselves with."

Keith laughed and said, "Oh, man! Don't tell me that you are scared! Don't worry, bro! I'll protect you!" He then put Jerry in a headlock and rubbed his knuckles into the top of his head.

The pair then heard a noise that startled them into putting a stop to the horseplay. Keith immediately released Jerry and said, "Did you hear that?"

"Yeah, I did. I couldn't tell which direction it came from though."

Suddenly angry, Keith said, "Okay. No more messing around. We need to find this fucker before he freaks out the girls. It'll be faster if we split up. You go that way and check the rooms and I'll go this way. We'll meet back here and go up to the attic if neither of us find him."

Jerry nodded yes, then the two did a fist bump and went their separate ways. After about five minutes the pair reconvened, both empty handed. They moved slowly to the steps leading to the third level. "You ready to do this?" Jerry asked.

"Yeah, let's get this over with!"

Back on the ground floor, Anna just ended her call with 911. "Well, what did they have to say?" Sabrina asked. "How much trouble are we in?"

Anna joined her on the couch and said, "Believe it or not, someone already called in the car accident. As for us being here…," Anna trailed off and made a face.

"Oh, no!" Sabrina said with a concerned look on her face. "How bad is it?"

Anna suddenly burst out into laughter. "Girl, you should see the look on your face! I have no idea how much trouble we're in. The dispatcher just said we need to stay put. A patrol car is on the way."

"You bitch! You've been hanging around Keith for too long!"

"Ha! Ha! You know, you may be right about that. But I can't help it. I love him." Anna then held out her left hand sporting a decent sized engagement ring.

"Oh my GOD!"

"Okay, wait! Before you curse me out again, we were going to tell you guys tonight, once we got to the house, but then Jerry's car died on us and…"

"It's okay, girl! I'm so happy for you both!"

"Thank you! We're so happy!"

The two women hugged briefly and then Sabrina said, "Okay, I want to hear all about it. Tell me everything!"

Anna laughed again and said, "Okay, okay! Well…" she then trailed off.

"What? What is it? What's wrong?"

"I don't know. I thought I saw something out of the corner of my eye."

"Are you trying to mess with me again?"

"No, girl I'm serious! It was right over…" She then started screaming, which of course alarmed Sabrina who looked to where Anna was pointing and saw a rat running along the base boards.

The two women leapt onto the couch and started screaming in unison.

The sound of the commotion reached Jerry and Keith, who were halfway up the stairs to the third floor. They looked at one another and Jerry said, "That sounds like…"

Keith finished the sentence by saying, "The girls!"

They quickly turned around and ran down the stairs to the second floor. Upon reaching the landing, they were about to head for the stairs leading to the ground floor when they heard a loud creak coming from behind them. They turned around and neither man was prepared for the behemoth standing before them.

Harold the Butcher stood at six feet, five inches tall and was every bit of three hundred and fifty pounds. He was completely bald and clean shaven with an ugly diagonal scar that ran from his scalp and over his face through his left eye down across his nose to his jaw line. He was one ugly motherfucker with massive hands, one of which was holding a machete. Each wrist still held the remains of his handcuffs as if he simply snapped them in two and was wearing them now as if they were bracelets. He was still wearing his cocoa-brown coveralls prison attire and brown leather work boots.

He was the closest to Keith, who took a step back and said, "Who the fuck are..." he didn't get a chance to finish. Without uttering a sound, Harold thrust the machete through Keith's mouth with enough force that the tip of the blade exited the back of his head.

"Keith!" Jerry screamed his friends' name in shock and disbelief.

Harold put a boot to Keith's chest and snatched the machete from the dead man's skull. As his body fell to the ground, Jerry spun on his heels and ran for the flight of stairs, screaming for the women to get out of the house.

Anna and Sabrina could not make out what Jerry was saying but they could hear loud racing footsteps. They jumped off the couch and ran to face the stairwell leading up to the second floor.

Anna yelled for Keith and Sabrina yelled out Jerry's name. They were about to head up when they heard this thump, thumping sound on the stairwell that grew louder and louder as it came closer.

Both women gasped and then screamed as they realized it was Jerry's head bouncing down the steps. Sabrina went into hysterics once the head came to rest looking up with now vacant eyes, it's mouth wide open as if it was in mid scream.

Anna screamed for Keith and then backed away from the steps once she saw Harold creeping down them. This time she screamed in pure terror at the mere sight of the madman. Before she could make a move, Harold hurled the machete straight at her. It struck her with enough force that she was impaled to the wall behind her.

Seeing Anna's now lifeless body go limp was enough to snap Sabrina out of her grief and into survival mode. She ran for the door and snatched it open with Harold hot on her tail. She made it outside into the still pouring rain and was greeted immediately with a sea of patrol cars and flashing lights. Officers had their weapons drawn and were pointing them directly at the door.

One of them yelled, "Get down!" and without hesitation Sabrina dropped to the cold wet ground and remained flat as possible.

Once Harold came running through the doorway another officer yelled, "Fire!" and every officer on the scene unloaded their weapons, essentially lighting Harold up. His body jerked to and fro with every striking bullet until eventually, he collapsed to the ground, not moving.

"Cease fire!" an officer yelled as Hernandez and Jackson raced to scoop up a visually shaken and distraught Sabrina.

"You're gonna be okay, miss," Officer Jackson said. "Officer Hernandez here is going to take you over there so you can get checked out."

He then walked over to Harold and used his foot to turn the body over so that it was face up.

Hernandez stopped and asked, "Is he dead?"

Harold suddenly opened his one good eye and tried to sit up, but Officer Jackson was well prepared and fired a single shot right into his forehead. "He is now."

Ralph pulled into the driveway of his home with a smile on his face. After turning the engine off, he grabbed the bouquet of flowers and a wrapped present from the passenger seat and exited his car. Upon entering his home, he was greeted with the delicious scent of whatever feast his wife was cooking up in the kitchen.

Pausing briefly in the dining room, he noticed the table was already set for dinner and a bottle of Merlot was open, allowing it to breathe. Candles also adorned the table along with red and white rose petals. "Man, she really went all out this year!" Ralph thought to himself. He paused outside the entrance to the kitchen to admire his wife from behind.

Ashley was wearing a red halter sleeveless mini dress and had a black apron tied around her waist. Her long auburn hair was in an elaborate upswept style, and she was wearing red heels. As dirty thoughts began to swirl around in his head, he involuntarily squeezed the wrapping around the flowers causing a loud crinkly sound.

Startled, Ashley spun around but quickly recovered at the sight of her husband. "Oh, my gosh! You scared me, Ralph! You shouldn't sneak up on a woman with a knife!" She smiled and laid the knife she was holding on the counter.

"I'm sorry beautiful! I was just admiring the view!" He closed the gap between them and gave his wife a passionate kiss.

Breaking free of the kiss, Ashley smiled and said, "All is forgiven. Now get yourself settled. Dinner is just about ready."

"Okay. But first, these are for you!" Ralph handed over the bouquet of lilies and peach roses, her favorite and the present.

"Thank you, sweetheart. I'll put these in water right away." She handed the present back to Ralph and then grabbed a crystalline vase. Going to the sink, she filled it halfway with water and then arranged the flowers to her liking. Once satisfied, she walked past Ralph to place the arrangement in the center of the dining room table.

Upon returning to the kitchen, she retrieved the present from Ralph and asked, "Should I open this now or wait until after dinner?"

"By all means. Please open it now."

Smiling and eager, she said, "Okay, if you insist!" Tearing open the wrapping and opening the large square box, she gasped. "Oh, my GOD, Ralph! It's beautiful! You shouldn't have!"

"Hey, nothing but the best for you, my love! May I...?"

Ashley quickly nodded as she held up the box for Ralph to retrieve the diamond eternity necklace encased in eighteen-carat white gold. She turned around as he placed the stunningly beautiful piece of jewelry around her neck and closed the clasp.

She had tears in her eyes as she turned around once more to face him. Smiling, he said, "You look absolutely amazing."

Throwing her arms around his neck, she said, "Thank you! I love it!"

"And I love you!" Kissing his wife again, he then said, "Okay, let me get out of this monkey suit and I'll be right back."

"Dinner will be ready and waiting. You don't get your present until dessert though!"

Ralph just smiled, nodded, and headed upstairs to their bedroom without saying another word.

Ashley waited until she was sure Ralph was upstairs before she let the smile and façade of happiness drain from her face. She then went about completing the dinner she was preparing.

Upon entering the master bedroom, Ralph undressed, throwing his suit and tie onto the back of a chair and the rest of his clothes into the hamper. He took a quick shower and dressed in a powder blue polo shirt and comfy black slacks. He found his favorite black loafers and slipped them on before heading back downstairs.

Once he reached the dining room, he saw that Ashley was already seated and patiently waiting for him. She had prepared filet mignon, seared scallops, asparagus, and garlic mashed potatoes. "Oh, my GOD, honey," he said, as he eagerly sat down across from her. "This looks and smells amazing! You really outdid yourself!"

"Thank you, sweetie. You only get to celebrate your ten-year anniversary once. I want tonight to be special." Ashley then held up her wine glass, and Ralph quickly mimicked the gesture as she said, "Happy anniversary darling."

Smiling, Ralph said, "Happy Anniversary Sweetheart!"

The couple clinked their glasses, took a sip, and then proceeded to enjoy their meal. When they were done, Ashley stood up and said, "I hope you saved room for dessert." She collected their plates as Ralph refilled their glasses with wine. Ashley went into the kitchen and returned carrying a triple-chocolate mousse cake adorned with red frosting crafted into decorative roses.

"Hon," Ralph began. "The cake is beautiful. You must have been in the kitchen all day putting this incredible meal together."

Sitting the cake down, Ashley cut a slice for her husband and said, "No, not really. I've been planning this evening for months now, so it was just a matter of following through on the execution." She placed the slice of cake with a clean fork in front of her husband and returned to her seat.

"Hey, aren't you going to have any?" Ralph took a bite and said, "Mmm... Oh, my GOD, this is so good, honey! It's delicious!"

"I'm glad you like it. I'm currently full, so maybe I'll have a slice later."

Ralph took a sip of wine before saying, "Well, you should have some. How did I get to be so lucky as to have such an amazing wife?" He then took another bite of the cake.

"Do you really feel that way, Ralph?"

"Yes. Of course, I do! Why would you ask me that?" Ralph sat his fork down with a concerned look on his face.

Ashley simply sighed, then pulled a large manilla envelope from underneath her and slid it across the table to Ralph. She then said, "Happy Anniversary, darling!"

Puzzled, Ralph picked up and opened the envelop, emptying its contents onto the table. A dozen or so of various sized photographs landed in front of him. "What is this?" he began and then gasped as he picked up a photo and recognized himself in a compromising position with another woman. All the pictures featured him and the same woman at different times and places doing things not meant for public consumption.

"Holy shit! How did you? I mean..." suddenly feeling whoozy, Ralph continued, "Whaa? What's happ... Did you... drug me..." He then face-planted into what remained of the slice of cake he was eating. He was out like a light.

When he awakened, he realized he was in his brightly lit basement. He had to blink a few times to allow his eyes time to adjust. Upon spotting his wife sitting calmly in a nearby chair, he tried to move and speak but couldn't because he was gagged and bound tightly to a chair, which was sitting inside a large metal tub next to a huge hole in their basement floor.

Ashley stood up calmly and walked over to stand in front of her husband before snatching the duct tape from his mouth.

"Jesus Christ, Ashley! What-the-fuck?!?! Untie me! What the hell is going on?"

"What's going on is that you've been fucking that bitch Madison behind my back for GOD knows how long and I've had it. You're done treating me like a fool."

"Come on baby. You're overreacting! Can't we talk about this?"

Ashley smiled and said, "Well now, I'm impressed. You're not even trying to deny it or say that it's over or that it meant nothing. Kudos to you. Of course, we can talk about it. It's not going to change anything though, but first, Bruno! You can bring her out now!"

Puzzled, Ralph said, "Bruno? Who the fuck is Bruno?"

Ashley laughed and said, "Hold on to your tighty-whities, sweetie. All will be revealed real soon. Ralph then saw the door to their storage and garage open and a big and burly man come through pushing a woman in a chair. She was also bound and gagged. The woman was placed in front of him in the same metal tub. It wasn't long before Ralph realized, in disbelief, that it was Madison. Her usually long and beautiful blonde hair looked unruly and matted. Streaks of mascara ran down her face as she had been crying profusely. She looked scared and just a little bit unhinged. Her eyes kept darting from him to Ashley and then this Bruno fella.

Bruno had to be every bit of six-foot three inches and all muscles. His dark green t-shirt and khaki pants fit the man like a second skin. He sported a stylish haircut, with his brown hair tapered on the sides and longer and wavy on top. His green eyes were set off with thick eyebrows and eyelashes and he was clean shaven with a dimpled chin.

Ashley placed a hand on Ralph's chin and ever so gently lifted his face so that he was looking up at her instead of at Madison. "You wanted to talk, so let's talk." She released him and walked over to stand beside Bruno before continuing. "You see, Bruno here is your replacement. I met him not long after I found out about your affair with this slut."

Madison began loudly murmuring and squirming in her chair.

"Oh, simmer down, whore!" Ashley said. "You'll get your chance to speak." Ashley returned her attention to Ralph. "I started seeing a therapist once I figured out that you had been cheating on our marriage. As is typical in these types of situations, I took all the blame upon myself. I thought I wasn't pretty enough, woman enough, perhaps negligent in some way. I was on the verge of killing myself and then I found out I was pregnant.

"What?" Ralph asked incredulously. "We're having a baby?"

Madison also looked on in disbelief and began crying again.

Ashley got into Madison's face and said, "Bitch! What are you crying about? I haven't even come for you yet!" She stood up straight again and returned her attention to her husband. "You and your side piece can calm down. I'm not having your baby. I got rid of it. Starting a family with you was everything I thought I wanted but you turned that dream into a nightmare. I didn't want to bring a child into the world under these circumstances.

Even though I knew this was the right decision for me, I was still devastated afterwards. After a particularly brutal therapy session, I didn't even make it to my car. I collapsed into a bawling mess on the floor near the elevators. The next thing I knew, I was being lifted effortlessly off the floor and carried to a sitting area. Bruno, without saying a word just held me until I was able to calm down."

"So, what?" Ralph asked, "You wanted to get back at me, so you started an affair with this ape?"

Bruno walked over and was about to slap the taste out of Ralph's mouth, but Ashley held up a hand to stop him. She pulled a large metal can from a shelf and handed it to him. This caused Bruno to smile. He accepted the can and went back to standing silently in his previous spot.

Ashley then said, "Actually, Bruno was quite the gentleman. He listened, which is so desperately what I needed at the time. He didn't judge me. He was there for me initially only as a friend. Eventually, as I grew to trust him and our friendship deepened, our relationship evolved into something magical."

Ashley sat back down and then said, "So what about you two? Care to share?" She reached down and picked up a glass of wine and took a sip as she looked from Madison to Ralph. She then looked up at Bruno and said, "Would you be a dear and remove the tape from her mouth? I really do want to hear what she has to say."

Bruno nodded and walked over to Madison. With no warning or hesitation, he swiftly snatched the tape from her mouth and moved back to his previous position.

Madison pleaded with Ashley, "What do you want from us? Please, just let us go!"

Smiling, Ashley said, "What I want, Lovelita, are answers to my questions. You knew he was married when you first got together didn't you? But you just didn't care. You wanted what you wanted and to hell with me or my feelings. So, what was the plan, hmm? Was this just supposed to go on endlessly?"

Madison looked timidly at Ralph but all he returned was a blank stare.

At this point Ashley had run out of patience and screamed, "Answer me, dammit! What the fuck were your plans with my husband?"

"Alright Ashley! Leave her alone!" Ralph said. "You've made your point!"

"No dear husband," Ashley said. "I have not even begun to make my point. You will know when I have."

It was at this time that Ashley gave Bruno a slight nod, which caused him to smile. He walked behind Madison and began to pour some of the contents from the metal can that he was holding over the top of her head.

Ralph became even more agitated and said, "What the hell is that supposed to mean? Hey! What are you doing to her? Get away from her?"

Madison meekly called out Ralph's name to which Ashley replied, "Honey, there isn't a damn thing that he can do for you."

"For Christ's sake Ashley!" Ralph yelled. "What is the point of all of this? Are we on fucking trial here?"

Ashley smiled, sat her glass of wine down and stood up happily. "Ding! Ding! Ding!" she said. "Give that man a cigar! You hit the nail on the head darling. You both are most absolutely on trial." She walked over to a shelf and pulled a mobile phone encased in a pink phone case. She held it up for the pair of hostages to see. "I present to you, exhibit A."

Madison's eyes widened in horror. She said, "That's my phone, bitch! What are you doing?"

Ashley ignored her and gave a slight smile and a nod to Bruno. He set the can down and grabbed her from behind, essentially putting her in a chokehold. He used his free hand to force open one of her eyes. Ashley held the phone up to Madison's face and unlocked the phone.

"Okay, now we're getting somewhere," Ashley said as she began scrolling through the phone.

"For the love of GOD, Ashley!" A now agitated Ralph yelled. "Stop this madness and let us go!" As he struggled, he felt the bonds around his hands begin to loosen, which gave him a sense of hope of getting out of the mess he found himself in.

"Patience, dear husband. This will all be over soon. Since you two insist on remaining tightlipped on your shenanigans, I figured I'd get to the truth by other means. So, let's see what we have here, shall we?"

Ashley slowly skimmed through the messages on the phone and said, "Okay, based on what I'm seeing here, it looks like you guys have been hot and heavy for a little over a year now. Of course, I could be wrong and this thing between the two of you could have been going on longer than that, but that's neither here nor there. I just found something interesting. Bruno, you're going to want to hear this one! It's a killer!"

Bruno looked intrigued and gave a wide smile.

Ashley continued, "So, Madison here sent this message to my dear devoted husband just a week ago. Now, it should also be noted that on this date, Ralph was supposed to be working late on a project with his team at the office. Anyway, the message reads, 'You were incredible as always. I miss you already! I can't wait for the day that you finally leave that bitch, and I can claim you as mine and mine alone. I ache for you. I yearn for you, and I burn for you!' Well," Ashley said as she closed the phone and put it back on the shelf. "Isn't that special? I tell you what, Madison. I'm so touched by your words, especially that last part, that I'm going to make that happen for you." She then pulled a box of matches from the shelf.

"What are you on about now Ashley?" Ralph said. "You're not making any sense."

"Oh, I'm sure everything is about to become crystal clear sweetheart," Ashley said as she pulled a matchstick and struck it against the box, igniting a flame. She then casually threw the lit match into the lap of a now horrified Madison who immediately became engulfed in flames from being doused in kerosene earlier.

Her screams were horrendous, and Ralph yelled, "Oh GOD! Oh GOD! What have you done, you psychotic bitch! You fucking killed her!" He began violently shaking in his chair until he was able to snatch an arm free although it was still attached to a now broken arm rest.

As Bruno tossed Madison's still engulfed remains into the hole, Ashley picked up the can of kerosene and poured its contents over Ralph. When she went to retrieve the matches, Bruno walked over to grab Ralph and lifted him effortlessly. In a last-ditch effort to save his own life, Ralph stabbed Bruno in the chest with the broken arm rest of the chair.

His miscalculated effort did not have the desired effect, however, as all he managed to do was throw Bruno off balance. Bruno was able to maintain his grip on Ralph even as he tumbled backwards into the hole with the still smoldering remains of Madison which promptly reignited.

"Bruno!" Ashley screamed as she ran to the edge of the hole.

A screaming Ralph, engulfed in flames, leapt forward and dragged Ashley kicking and screaming back into the hole with the rest of them where they all burned until there was nothing left but charred bones.

Black Cherry

It's a warm summer evening, around eleven pm in the Chestnut Hill section of Philadelphia. A house full of friends are gathered around the dining room table singing happy birthday to the guest of honor, Dalton Whitlock.

After the last note, everyone cheered and raised their cups to toast the birthday boy. Someone yelled, "Speech!" And soon, the sentiment echoed amongst the guests until Dalton finally relented and gestured for everyone to settle down.

"I love you guys! Thanks so much for coming and helping to make my day special! I'm really going to miss each and every one of you! Cheers!"

Everyone cheered, took a sip of their drinks, and then took turns to hug or shake Dalton's hand. Someone began handing out slices of cake, chocolate/vanilla marble with cream cheese frosting. Just as Dalton took a bite Colter and Zaiden walked up with somber looks on their faces.

"Come on guys, I'm not dying, I'm just moving. You'll both still be my best buds."

"Yeah," Zaiden said, "but you'll be three thousand miles away. It won't be the same around here without you."

"I think what he means to say, is," Colter began, "Is that we're going to miss you man!"

"I'm going to miss you guys too! Look at it this way, you now have somewhere to go on vacation. Trust me, you boys will fall in love with Palm Springs!"

Just then the three men heard a commotion coming from the living room. They went to investigate and saw a small gathering engaged in a slightly heated debate. "Hey, what's going on in here that has everyone so riled up?" Dalton asked.

Octavia stepped forward and said, "It's Maurice trying to scare us with some scary tale bullshit. I was telling him that we're not in college anymore and we're not sitting around a campfire."

"Scary tale? What are you up to now Maurice?" Zaiden asked.

Maurice said, "I did not make this up. I was just explaining that it was on the news today about the anniversary of Cheryl Black's death. They were saying it's been thirty years and her case is still unsolved."

"Cheryl Black? Why does that name sound familiar?" Dalton asked.

Colter jumped in and said, "You remember! We used to talk about it all the time when we were kids. We overheard our parents talking about it, but they weren't calling her by her proper name, it was something else..."

Zaiden jumped in and said, "Black Cherry! They all used to call her Black Cherry!"

"Yeah, that's it!" Maurice said. There's even a rhyme that they made up about her."

Octavia put her hands on her hips and said, "Are you guys serious? This shit is for real?"

It was at this point that Maya stepped forward and said, "Yes. It is real. I remember it now. I even remember the rhyme.

Black Cherry, Cherry Black
Fell down the stairs and broke her back
No one noticed and worst of all
Was she pushed or did she fall?
Seek the truth if that's your goal
Just chant her name and lose your soul

"That's just awful!" everyone turned to see that Jade, who had just spoken was on the verge of tears. "Is that really what happened to her? She fell down the stairs?"

"Yes," Maurice said. "They ruled it an accident, but there was always a lingering doubt because she was at a frat party in North Philly. The house was packed with partygoers and yet no one came forward. They questioned everyone but to no avail. Eventually, the case was dropped and closed as an unfortunate accident."

"But that's not where the story ends," Zaiden jumped in. "Rumor has it that one of the fraternity brothers roofied and raped her. When she tried to escape, the theory goes that someone pushed her down the steps. She didn't really break her back; it was her neck when she landed at the base of the staircase. The fraternity treated the whole thing as a joke and one drunken night made a party game out of the incident and began chanting her name. That's where the nick name Black Cherry comes from."

"Those sick bastards!" Maya said.

"No worries, Maya," Colter said. "They all got what was coming to them."

"What do you mean?" Octavia asked.

"Now, this is the part that I definitely remember because it was so bizarre," Dalton said. "Every single frat brother from that night died one by one under mysterious, unexplained circumstances. Some were ruled suicide and others tragic accidents."

"Stop playing with us!" Octavia said. "Now ya'll are just fucking with us!"

Dalton held up a finger, ran into his den and came back with his laptop. He quickly sat down on his couch and pulled up the fraternity from the year of the tragedy. The small group gathered around him as he displayed the pictures of about twenty fraternity brothers.

He looked up at Octavia and said, "Pick a name, any name." She pointed to the smiling image of Joseph Childs. Dalton googled the name and pulled up the first article that popped up. It showed an image of a heavily damaged motorcycle and an eighteen-wheeler.

The article headline: "Motorcycle driver killed instantly upon head-on collision with tractor trailer, his body went through the grill of the truck."

Octavia gasped as Dalton closed the story. Jade then pointed to another picture, Milton Jeffries. Dalton googled him and again opened the first article. It read, "Young man dies after unfortunate elevator malfunction. The car plummeted seventeen stories to the basement."

"Oh, my GOD!" Jade said. "You're telling me, that all of those fraternity brothers are dead?" This really happened?"

"That's what I was trying to tell you all earlier," Maurice said. "Before you all jumped down my throat. This shit is no joke."

"But you do have to admit," Maya said. "Isn't it a little cray-cray to think that just because they did some sick chant that, what? This Black Cherry chick came back and killed them all? Didn't they already do that movie? Candyman, Bloody Mary?"

Dalton closed his laptop and set it aside. He leaned back and said, "What are you trying to say, Maya? After everything you've just learned, you still think that what happened was just some silly coincidence?"

"I don't know what I think, just yet. I mean ghosts aren't real, are they? They can't really harm you or make you do stuff. I'm sorry, I just don't think I believe in that sort of thing."

"I'm gonna call your bluff!" Maurice said. "If you don't believe, then let's do it! Let's call her right now!"

"Are you fucking nuts?!?" Colter said. "I'm not doing that shit! I'm not fucking with no ghosts!"

Octavia quickly chimed in with, "Yeah, I second that emotion!"

Dalton looked at Jade and said, "What about you?"

Looking slightly uncomfortable, Jade waited a beat and said, "I guess I'm down. If Maya's doing it, I'm in. What about you?"

Dalton shrugged and said, "Sure, why not? You only live once, right?"

"That's what I'm afraid of!" Octavia said. "You guys are fucking nuts!"

"Come on," Zaiden said, "You don't really believe some ghost is going to appear and kill you, do you? I'm in. I'll do it!"

"My man!" Dalton said as he stood up and clapped Zaiden on the back. "Alright, everyone, lets gather in front of the mirror in the dining room. Colter, Octavia, you guys coming?"

The pair looked at each other, shrugged, and nodded yes. Everyone gathered with the rest of the guests in the dining room when someone asked, "Hey, what's going on?"

Maurice said, "We're playing a ghost game. We're going to call on Black Cherry to make an appearance here tonight."

"No shit!" Someone else yelled. "Cool! Let's do it!"

Jade asked, "Okay, so how does this work?"

"It's just like the movies," Maurice said. "Just look into the mirror and say Black Cherry five times and she's supposed to appear. Everyone ready?"

In unison the group of partygoers yelled, "Yes!" and turned to face the mirror.

Maurice then said, "Okay, on the count of three we'll begin. One...two...three!"

Everyone repeated the name and on the fifth go around there was a moment of silence when suddenly the lights went out. The crowd began to murmur when just as quickly the lights came back on and then someone screamed. Everyone turned to look at the screamer who was frantically pointing towards the living room. Everyone turned again to face the direction of the living room and that's when pandemonium erupted. Standing there in a white tattered dress was a frighteningly unkempt and pale woman who looked like she had just crawled thru the swamp.

People were screaming and crawling all over themselves in search of the exit. Unable to keep themselves in check any longer, Maurice and Dalton broke out into a fit of laughter. "Hold... hold on everyone! This is just a joke! Ha, ha! I'm sorr… I'm so sorry but it was Maurice's idea, and I just couldn't resist!"

There was nervous laughter from the crowd as everyone tried to regain their composure. "This is Joanne," Maurice said as he walked up to the ghost performer. She smiled broadly and took a bow. "Oh, my GOD you guys! That was priceless!"

Jade walked over and punched Maurice in the arm.

"Oww! What you do that for?"

"You assholes! Octavia literally just pissed herself!" Everyone turned to see that the now embarrassed Octavia was sporting a large wet stain in the front of her shorts.

Joanne said, "Oh, shit! I'm so sorry. I brought a couple of things with me to change into and I believe I have a skirt that will fit you. Come on, let's get you cleaned up."

Octavia nodded and moved to follow her when both Maurice and Dalton apologized. If looks could have killed both men would be dead right now.

Maurice waited until the pair were upstairs and out of earshot before he said, "Ooohweee! She is pissed! No pun intended!"

"You dick!" Maya said. "I was on the verge of peeing myself as well. What possessed you guys to terrorize us like that?"

"Yeah, man," Colter said. "You got us good! I'm supposed to be your best friend and I didn't even know what you guys were planning."

Dalton put a hand on Colter's shoulder and said, "I love you man, but you cannot keep a secret to save your life. I'm sorry but we never would have been able to pull this off if you'd known."

"Besides," Maurice said, "We wanted this to be a party to remember. You know people will be talking about this for months if not years!"

Maya then said, "So, none of this real? All of it was made up bullshit?"

"Oh, no," Dalton said. "The story of Cheryl Black is very real as well as all those dead fraternity brothers. We did not make any of that up."

"And today really is the thirtieth anniversary of her death," Maurice added.

Jade then said, "Well, if everything you told us about that poor girl is true, what if we really did just summon her vengeful spirit?"

In the upstairs master suite, Octavia exited the bathroom freshened up and wearing a black mini skirt. "Thank you. The skirt fits perfectly. I'll get it back to you as soon as possible."

"No rush, hon," Joanne said as she entered the bathroom. "It's the least I could do. I really am sorry. I don't even know why I agreed to do it." She began to wash the ghoulish makeup off her face.

"Are you coming to the club with the rest of us?"

Joanne dried her face off and said, "Most definitely. I wouldn't miss it! The limo should be here any minute."

"Okay then. I'm gonna head back downstairs. Thanks again for the skirt."

"No problem. I'll be down in five." Joanne put the tattered dress in her overnight bag and dressed in a black t-shirt and white jeans. She slipped on some black pumps and returned to the bathroom mirror to apply some makeup. After searching for and finding her lipstick, she was about to apply it when she realized it wasn't her reflection staring back at her.

Gasping, she took a huge step backwards slamming against the back of the bathroom door. Daring to look again in the mirror, she once again recognized herself and breathed a huge sigh of relief. Shaking the jitters off, she chalked it up to an overactive imagination and finished applying her lipstick.

She tossed the wig she was wearing in her bag, teased her hair out and once she was satisfied with her look, placed her bag in Dalton's closet and joined her friends downstairs. "Hey, Dalton," She said, I hope you don't mind but I threw my bag into your closet, so I don't have to drag it around with me."

"Not a problem at all," he said.

Maurice walked up and said, "You look amazing! Thanks again for doing that for us. It was great!"

Joanne cast a casual glance over to Octavia before responding, "Yeah, well, I ought to have my head examined for agreeing to do it. I had no idea we'd get the reaction we did."

Maya stepped up and said, "Don't you dare blame yourself. Maurice and Dalton did a really good job of setting us up."

Dalton and Maurice smiled and gave each other a high five.

"She's right," Octavia said. "No one here is mad at you. But mark my words, we're going to get these jerks back!"

Joanne looked around and said, "Where is everyone?"

Zaiden said, "They all left for the club and said they would meet us there."

Just then they heard a car horn. Colter opened the front door and said, "Okay everyone, the limo's here."

"You all go on," Dalton said. "I'm gonna grab a couple bottles of champagne, lock up and I'll be out in a second."

"Alright," Joanne said. "I am more than ready for a drink! Let's get this party started!"

Octavia, Maya and Jade cheered in unison and joined her as she made her way outside. Maurice and Colter quickly followed but Zaiden stayed behind and closed the door.

He walked up to Dalton and said, "Hey, hold up a sec." He grabbed Dalton by the waist and said, "I probably won't get another chance to be alone with you tonight, so I'm taking the opportunity to do this." He then planted a long, sensuous kiss on Dalton's lips. After a beat he broke free and said, "I must admit that I'm still having a hard time dealing with this. I can't believe you're leaving me. I understand your reasons, I really do."

Dalton took a step back and said, "I did ask you to come with me and the offer still stands. You can feel free to come out of the closet and live your life, with me."

Zaiden put his hands in his pockets and looked down at the floor. He was about to say something when they heard the horn from the limo sound.

Dalton quickly grabbed two bottles of champagne from the kitchen and said, "Look, we can talk about this later. You still have a few days to decide and no matter what, just know that I will always love you. That will never change."

Zaiden grabbed the bottles, gave a quick smile and a nod, then headed for the door. The pair exited the house and once Dalton locked up; they joined their friends in the limo. Everyone had a glass in hand and Maurice said, "Come on slow pokes! Pop that shit!"

Dalton laughed as he and Zaiden each opened a bottle as the limo pulled away. No one noticed the body of one of the partygoers lying in between two parked cars as the vehicle drove down the street. The eyes had been completely removed, leaving behind two black holes.

Shortly thereafter, they arrived at the afterhours club known as Blue Velvet. There was a line wrapped around the block to get in, but Dalton and his friends walked up to the doorman who smiled broadly once he recognized the birthday boy.

"Hey, Dalton! Good to see you! Happy Birthday! Most of your guests are already inside in the VIP section."

Dalton shook the man's hand and said, "Thank you, Cedric! You're looking good as always!"

"Hey, I'm just trying to keep up with you!" Cedric laughed as he unhooked the velvet rope and gestured for the group to enter.

The club was cavernous, three stories high, not counting the basement level and had three bars. Mirrors adorned one wall from floor to ceiling and a disco ball was centered over the large dance floor, which was already filled with people dancing the night away. The music was loud and pulsating.

Joanne grabbed Maurice and said, "Come on! This is my song, and you owe me a dance!"

Maurice laughed and said, "Ok, beautiful!" he looked at the rest of the group and said, "I'll catch up with you guys!"

Everyone nodded and headed for the VIP section. The rest of the party cheered and immediately handed out shots to the late arrivals. After a beat, people began breaking up into smaller groups, some headed towards the dance floor, and others left to wander the club. Eventually, the only ones left were Dalton, Zaiden, and Colter.

Colter leaned forward and said, "Okay, spill it. I know something's up with you two, so what's going on?"

At that moment, Joanne was pulling Maurice off the dance floor. "Hey, gorgeous. What are you up to now?"

"Just follow me!" She smiled as she led him away from the crowd by the hand past the bathrooms to a door. She tried the door and smiled broadly when it turned easily in her hand. After pushing it open, she turned to Maurice and said, "Okay, come on. Quickly, before someone sees us!"

Maurice complied and allowed Joanne to lead him down the stairs into the basement. They walked past boxes of liquor, empty beer kegs and racks of assorted barware. Finally, they arrived at another door. Joanne tried the door handle and squealed with delight to find that it too, was open.

"Yes!" She exclaimed as she pulled a now excited Maurice into what appeared to be an abandoned office. The light was extremely faint, but they could see a couch, a desk and desk lamp, some cabinets and not much else.

"Okay, mmph!" Maurice was about to ask a question, but Joanne put a finger to his lips.

"All you need to know is that I want you and I want you now!" She pulled his shirt up and over his head and tossed it on the desk. She undid his belt buckle and opened his jeans before forcefully pulling them down.

Smiling mischievously, she said, "Oh, you naughty boy! Going commando, I see! And obviously so very ready for what I have in store for you!"

Back in the VIP lounge, Dalton and Zaiden exchanged nervous glances in response to Colter's question. Zaiden gave Dalton a look and without saying a word, asked for permission to spill the beans.

Dalton's response was a slight shrug with a tilt of the head and a nod giving the go ahead.

Zaiden poured himself a shot of tequila and downed it quickly. He looked at Colter, who was patiently awaiting a response. Swallowing hard, he leaned forward and said, "Okay, the truth of the matter is, Dalton and I have been seeing each other for about a year now." Zaiden paused to look at Dalton before he continued, "And I am helplessly, deeply, madly in love with this man!" After that admission, a single tear slowly slid down his cheek.

Dalton reached out and gently wiped the tear away. He slowly turned Zaiden's face towards his own and said, "Hey, I love you too!" The two men kissed passionately before remembering where they were and tried quickly to regain their composure. They turned to face Colter and were both equally shocked and surprised to see him grinning from ear to ear.

"Umm, why is he smiling?" Zaiden asked.

"I have no idea," Dalton said. "Colter, what's up with you?"

Still smiling, Colter leaned back against the couch and crossed his legs and spread his arms over the back of the couch. "Come on, guys! I already knew," he said. "You both thought you were being slick, but you forget that I know you. We've been friends since our toddler days, so you'd be hard-pressed to put one over on me. Well, except for that Black Cherry scare earlier, anyway."

Dalton then said, "Well, if you knew that we were together, why didn't you ever say anything?"

"I didn't feel that it was my place, and it wasn't any of my business. I was initially hurt but figured you guys would come around eventually. It took for me to nudge you guys, but here we are." Colter than pointed a finger at Dalton and said, "It wasn't that long ago that you said I couldn't keep a secret."

Dalton stood up and said, "Man, I am so sorry. You two are my best friends and if it had been up to me…"

Zaiden then stood up and interrupted, "It's all my fault. I was, no, I still am coming to terms with everything. With my feelings and what that means."

"Now it was Colter's turn to stand up. He walked closer to his friends and said, "Hey, it's all good. No apologies necessary. I'm here for whatever you guys need. I gotcha back!"

Returning to the basement, Maurice was laying blissfully on his back cradling Joanne in his arms. "So, tell me gorgeous, was this on your bucket list or something? How did you even know about this spot?"

Smiling, Joanne repositioned herself so that she could look Maurice in the eyes. She was about to respond, when they heard a sharp scratching sound coming from the corner of the room. The couple bolted upright and leapt from the couch, scrambling for their clothes.

"What the fuck was that?" Maurice asked. "Who's there?"

Joanne quickly pulled up and fastened her jeans. "I don't see anything," she said. "Do you have your phone?"

Maurice pulled on his shirt and said, "Yeah, I do. Hold on a sec." He activated the light on his phone and slowly scanned the room. "I don't see…" he stopped midsentence and dropped his phone upon feeling cold and clammy fingers caress both sides of his face. The last thing he feels is a tightened grip and then nothingness as his head is forcefully and swiftly snapped to face the opposite direction.

"Maurice?" Joanne dropped to her knees to the grab the phone and quickly stood up. She aimed the light from the phone in Maurice's direction just in time to see his body fall to the ground. Standing there in his place was the real vengeful spirit of Cheryl Black. She looked even more grotesque and frightening than any make up Joanne could have come up with.

The ghoul's hair was animated and moved freely about her head. Her eyes glowed a sickly yellow and the skin was a ghastly gray. Her mouth was black and twisted into a fierce snarl.

Knowing it was futile, Joanne yelled Maurice's name and then spun on her heals and bolted from the room. She ran towards the staircase and was only a few feet away when she tripped over a bottle that seemed to come from nowhere. She twisted her ankle as a result and hit the basement floor hard. Groaning and in pain, she turned over onto her back just in time to see a case of alcohol hovering above her head. She let out a bloodcurdling scream just as the box plummeted to the ground, smashing her head in the process.

Octavia, Jade and Maya filed into the ladies' room. Octavia made a beeline into one of the stalls while Jade and Maya walked over to the sinks and mirrors. Jade reached into her purse for mascara while Maya reapplied some lipstick.

"Octavia," Jade began, "Who was that hot guy you were dancing with? I've never seen him before."

"Oh. His name is Nick. We've gone out on a couple of dates."

"What?" Maya said as she spun around to face the stall. "Bitch! Have you been holding out on us?"

Octavia laughed and said, "No. I didn't want to say anything until there was something to talk about, but guys, I really like him! He's a really cool guy and he treats me like a queen. I asked him to meet us here so I could introduce him to everybody."

"That's awesome girl!" Maya said. "I'm so happy for you and I can't wait to meet him. Isn't that awesome Jade? Our sis has gone and found herself a boyfriend."

When Jade didn't respond, Maya turned to her friend and said, "Jade? Are you okay? What's wrong? You look like you've seen a ghost."

Jade still did not respond. She looked absolutely petrified and her lips began to tremble.

"Girl what's gotten into you?" Maya asked as she followed Jade's eyeline to face the mirror and that's when she screamed. Staring back at her was the angry spirit of Cheryl Black.

The entity threw her hands forward and the glass of the mirror shattered into shards and quickly levitated above the sinks. Before either girl could respond they were impaled with multiple pieces of the glass and fell to the floor, dead upon impact.

Octavia quickly pulled up her skirt and said, "Jade? Maya? What's happening?" She pushed open the stall door and screamed upon seeing the remains of her friends.

"No! No!" she cried. She was about to bend down to check on them and that's when she saw something out of the corner of her eye. She stood up just in time to see Cheryl step out of one of the mirrors. Octavia screamed again and flew out of the bathroom as fast as her feet could carry her. She ran in the direction of the dance floor and tried screaming for help, but the music was too loud.

She didn't see Nick or anyone else she recognized on the dance floor, so she made a beeline for the VIP Lounge. So grateful to see the guys still there, she practically collapsed into Colter's arms completely out of breath.

"Hey," Colter began as he eased her onto the couch. "Octavia? What's wrong?"

Just then, Nick arrived and asked, "Hey! What's going on? Octavia?"

Dalton, Colter, and Zaiden in unison said, "Who are you?"

"He's my boyfriend," Octavia said. "We have to get the fuck out of here and I mean right now. Black Cherry is real, and she just killed Maya and Jade!"

"Confused, Nick said, "Black Cherry?"

The guys ignored Nick and Colter said, "What are you talking about? Where are Maya and Jade?"

Octavia stood up then and screamed, "They are fucking dead! That bitch killed them, and she came out of the mirror and now she's after me!"

Colter looked up at Zaiden and Dalton who appeared to be just as confused as he was.

Suddenly, they heard a loud crash on the dance floor. The music stopped and then the screaming erupted. People were stampeding towards the exit door. Nick took Octavia's hand and they quickly headed for the exit as well.

Zaiden, Dalton, and Colter moved closer to the dance floor to look for answers and each stopped dead in their tracks upon recognizing the now dead body of Christopher, a friend of theirs who was at Dalton's house earlier for the party. He was lying face up, spreadeagle with a pool of blood oozing out from the back of his head.

Standing over his body was the very real vengeful spirit now known as Black Cherry. She took her time looking at each one of them as if deciding who would be her next victim. The piercing glare was more than enough to send chills up the spines of the men. The sense of dread and fear were so great, that each man felt cemented in place. Neither of them could move, that is until Cedric, the doorman came in and screamed their names.

"Fellas! What the hell are you doing? Get the fuck out of here now! The police have already been called and are on their way! Let's go!" Just then he spotted Black Cherry and said, "What the fuck is that?"

Suddenly finding their footing, the men ran towards the door and Zaiden said, "That's an angry ghost that wants to kill us!"

Cedric then said, "Oh, hell no! They don't pay me enough for this shit!" He quickly exited the building but tried to hold the door open. The men almost made it, but the door slammed closed in front of them with enough force that it broke Cedric's arm.

As Cedric cried out in pain, Nick, who witnessed the incident said, "Octavia, I don't think your friends are going to make it out of there. I'm so sorry. He lifted his hand that was holding hers to kiss it when he realized that, while he was still holding her hand, Octavia was no longer attached to it. He spun around and screamed looking for the rest of her, but she was nowhere to be found.

THE CHILD

The full moon illuminated the night sky in Philadelphia as heavy, fluffy snowflakes fell from above. A group of men were gathered late night behind a building on Penn's Landing. Muffled grunts could be heard as fists pummeled flesh from all angles. Upon hitting the ground, the recipient of the beat down was then kicked hard in the face, sending teeth and blood across the no longer pristine white snow on the ground.

"Jesus, Rick!" Donald said as he touched his friend on the shoulder. "You're gonna kill 'em! He's down. I think he's had enough!"

Rick, the self-elected leader of the group spun around in anger and got up in Donald's face. He was spitting mad as he yelled, "I'll say when this cocksucker has had enough! Understand me? Do you have a problem with that?"

Donald quickly nodded and said, "No boss. No problem."

Rick then addressed the rest of the group, that consisted of Bradley, Stephen, and Cody, "Any of you have something to add?" Without saying a word, all the men in unison nodded their heads no. "Good! That's what I thought!"

Jimmy, the unfortunate man on the ground spat out more blood, then turned to face his tormentor. "I'm sorry, Rick! I had no choice. They had me up against a wall."

Rick bent down and punched the man again. He said, "You betrayed us, Jimmy! You did have a choice. Now they're after all of us. For that, I'm afraid your actions are unforgivable!" Rick then pulled out a gun and pointed it at Jimmy's face. Jimmy cried out in protest and begged for his life, but to no avail. The ensuing gunshot echoed in the night as Rick squeezed the trigger.

A plume of smoke arose from the bullet hole in the now deceased's forehead as Rick stood up and spit on his former comrade. "That's for selling us out, you piece of shit!"

Suddenly, there was a loud clanging sound coming from behind the group causing everyone to quickly spin around to locate the source of the noise. They saw a disheveled child looking terrified standing there in the cold without a coat on.

"Oh, for Christ's sake! It's a kid!" Cody yelled.

"I don't give a fuck! He's seen too much!" Rick said. "Grab him!"

The kid then took off and ran up Christopher Columbus Boulevard with the men in hot pursuit. He was a few yards away when he slipped and took a tumble. Rick took advantage of the opportunity. He stopped and aimed his weapon at the child. Just as he squeezed the trigger, Donald intervened and pushed Rick's arm upward.

This only made Rick angrier, who now leveled his gun at Donald's head. In a tight, controlled voice and through gritted teeth, Rick said, "Give me one good reason why I shouldn't blow your fucking brains out right now!"

Donald threw his hands up and said, "Come on, Rick! That boy is only seven, maybe eight years old. Are we really going to execute a child? Is that what we're about now? I'm sure he's scared shitless and just needs some help. He's no threat to us!"

Stephen walked up and said, "Come on Rick. You know he's right. If we throw the kid a couple bucks and get him cleaned up, he'll probably be more of an asset than a hindrance."

This seemed to get through to Rick as he lowered the gun and said, "Fine!"

Donald lowered his hands and exhaled, not realizing until that moment that he was holding his breath in anticipation of what was about to happen next.

Rick put his gun away and said, "I supposed now you yahoos want to adopt the brat too! Anyone see where he went? The little fucker got away thanks to Donald."

Bradley said, "I saw him duck into that abandoned warehouse up ahead."

"Good! Let's go find him and have a nice long chat!"

The men slowly made their way to the four-story building and looked for an entrance. Bradley went to a door and said, "This is where I saw him enter." He tried it and the door opened easily. He held it open until everyone was inside and then closed it as quietly as he could.

"I can't see shit!" Cody said as he pulled out his cellphone to use as a light source. The rest of the men did the same.

Bradley whistled and said, "This place is huge! How the fuck are we supposed to find this kid in the dark?"

"Slowly and methodically," Rick said. "Looks to me like this place has four floors, not including the basement. I want Stephen and Donald to check the top two floors. I'm sure there's a stairwell around here somewhere. Bradley and Cody, you guys check this floor and the second. Meanwhile, I'll make my way to the basement. If any you find that..." Rick hesitated for a second before continuing, "That kid, bring him here to the first floor and call the rest of us to meet back here."

Bradley then said, "And what if we don't find him?"

Rick aimed the light from his phone at his own face for emphasis before saying, "Failure is not an option! Now let's go! I don't want to be here all fucking night!"

The men split up, with Stephen and Donald staying close to and walking along the walls until they finally came across a wrought iron stairwell. Once they were about halfway up and Donald felt like they were out of earshot of the other men, he said, "Is it just me, or is Rick becoming more and more unhinged? Thanks, by the way, for saving my life back there."

"No problem, man. And it's not just you! I just about shit myself when I thought he was going to shoot that kid! You were the only one brave enough to do something about it."

"Yeah, I don't know what came over me, but I couldn't let him do it. I've been feeling antsy for a while now but tonight just cemented it for me. Rick killing Jimmy tonight and almost possibly killing this kid, I can't do it anymore. After tonight, I'm out!"

Stephen stopped walking and said, "What? You know Rick would go ballistic! What are you going to say to him?"

Donald stopped walking too and said, "Not a damn thing! You know there's no reasoning with him. He'll see it as a betrayal. After we are done with this fiasco tonight, I'll proceed as if everything is normal. Tomorrow, I take off for Mexico to live out the rest of my days."

Stephen looked at Donald and said, "You're serious, aren't you?"

"As a heart attack!"

"Well, if you'll have me, I want in on that plan!"

"What? Seriously?"

"Yeah, man! I'm over this shit too!"

Donald laughed and said, "That's awesome! I would love the company!"

"Cool! Let's keep this between us and not say anything to Bradley or Cody."

"Aww, hell no! You don't have to worry about me saying diddly to those two knuckleheads. They are drinking every drop of Rick's kool-aid."

"Truth!"

The pair finally reached the top of the fourth floor and agreed to split, one going left and the other, right. Neither man realized that they were being watched the whole time. The little boy quietly scampered off for the lower floors.

At the same time, Bradley and Cody were busy searching the second floor together, opting not to split up. "So," Bradley was saying, "That's pretty fucked up about Jimmy, huh? I liked the motherfucker."

"Yo! I tried to warn him, man!" Cody said. I told him that if he was in a jam, he needed to talk to Rick. I said he didn't have to talk to me if he didn't want to, but he should talk to Rick at least. He didn't listen, so he got what he got."

"That's just cold, man."

"Hey, it is what it is and if Donald isn't careful, his ass may be next. What the fuck was he thinking going up against Rick like that? Twice tonight, no less. He must have a death wish!"

"I see your point but killing an innocent child? You would have been okay with Rick shooting this kid?"

Cody simply shrugged his shoulders, causing Bradley to nod his head in disbelief. The pair walked along silently for a bit, casting the light from their phones from side to side to perform a sweep of the area. Finding nothing, they descended back down to the first floor to continue their search.

"Man! What I wouldn't give for a cold brew right about now!" Bradley said. "This shit has gotten old, really quick!"

"I hear ya, man!" Cody said, "But the sooner we find this brat, the better for all of us."

"Yeah, maybe not so much for him!"

"Hey!" Cody said, grabbing Bradley's arm. "I think I just saw him!"

"Where?"

"Follow my light! Over there in the corner!"

Bradley did as Cody asked and sure enough, there was the little boy. He was standing next to a door. He snatched it open and ran through it.

"Hey, kid!" Cody yelled as he and Bradley took off after him. "We just want to talk! Nobody's going to hurt you!"

They reached the door and went into the room. There were racks and racks of rusted, empty shelving. Bradley closed the door behind them as they did a sweep of the room.

"Come on out little boy," Bradley said. "We just want to talk, maybe get you something to eat. I bet you're hungry, yeah?"

The pair were met with nothing but silence. "Where the hell could he have gotten off to now?" Cody asked. "I don't see any other exits from here, do you?"

"No," Bradley said. "I don't see any other doors or windows for that matter. He must be here somewhere."

At that moment they both heard a noise behind them, near the door they had just entered through. They spun around simultaneously and aimed their lights at the boy who was standing there watching them with a big smile on his face. Combined with the intensity in which he was staring at them both made for an unsettling experience.

"Um, Cody," Bradley said as he took a step backwards. "This kid is creeping me the hell out. I mean, what the fuck? He doesn't look scared of us as all."

"Seriously, Bradley?" Cody said. "He's just a fucking kid!"

Suddenly, the kid's eyes lost their pupils and went from white to a glowing, neon red causing Cody to now take a step back as well.

He exclaimed, "What the hell!" just as the kid's body seemed to erupt. There was a loud and wet slurping sound as the body of the child disappeared and standing in his place was a seven-foot creature with a triangular head and six blood-red eyes, with three on each side of its face.

The skin was scaly and milky-white. Its wide mouth displayed rows of razor-like teeth with a black serpent's tongue easing in and out repeatedly. The creature did not have arms, perse, but three long tentacles protruding from each side of its torso. Each tentacle displayed disc-like suckers and the suckers themselves had teeth as well. The torso and legs were slim put powerful and each foot displayed three toes with black talons.

The shapeshifter was a terrifying sight to behold, and Bradley and Cody stood rooted to the spot, unable to comprehend and believe in what they were seeing. The creature suddenly crouched and took a step forward. Its tentacles whipped forward at lightning speed attaching itself to Bradley's torso and two attaching to either side of his face, with the suckers burrowing painfully beneath his skin.

Bradley screamed, "Aahh! Cody help me! It hurts! It fucking hurts!"

But Cody remained unmoving. That is until the creature's torso opened up. The opening was diamond-shaped which displayed even more teeth. Bradley entered this opening feet first and the teeth went straight to work causing Bradley's screams to reach several decibels higher as he was slowly being eaten alive.

The effect of Bradley's blood hitting him in the face was the catalyst that Cody needed to break him out of the trance he was in. He then screamed but made no move to save his friend. Instead, he ran around the scene and out the door. As soon as he crossed the threshold, he yelled out in pain and fell to the floor. He turned over on his back and saw that there was one of the creature's tentacles wrapped around his ankle. One of the sucker's went to work burrowing into his flesh, causing him to scream out in agony. He managed to pull his gun and began firing at it repeatedly until it released him.

He tried to get up, but he could not put his weight on the one leg, which was bleeding profusely. He managed to crawl a few feet before the creature grabbed him again and dragged him kicking and screaming back into the room where Bradley met his grisly end.

Donald and Stephen, who were now on the third floor, heard the gun shots and raced to get back to the first floor. Upon reaching the ground floor, Donald, who was clearly agitated said, "So help me GOD, if those motherfuckers just executed a child!"

Stephen pulled his gun and said, "Let's keep our heads until we know what's going on."

"Agreed," Donald said, as he pulled his gun as well.

The pair began scanning the floor with the light from their phones. They spread out but not too far from each other. Stephen was the first to reach the area where Cody was dragged and spotted the blood on the ground. He called for Donald to join him, who practically sprinted over. They followed the blood trail into the room only to find even more blood.

"What the hell could have happened in here?" Donald asked. "Something doesn't seem right. I mean, Rick can be a sick son-of-a-bitch, but I don't believe he would torture or even massacre that kid. Not like this."

"I agree. Even if he was determined to shoot the kid, this seems like way too much blood."

"Alright. He said he was going to check out the basement. Since we haven't run into Cody or Bradley, we have to assume that they are with him."

Stephen nodded in agreement and the pair went in search of the entrance to the lower level.

Meanwhile, Rick, oblivious to the goings on above him, was just about done with his search of the basement when he happened upon a double-door entrance. It was unlocked so he entered the room to find what appeared to be a hangar and, to his surprise, something he could only classify as a spaceship.

It was unlike anything he had ever seen before. The metal had a bluish-grey tint. It was two stories tall and about a city block long. The front of the ship was angular, rounded at the tip with a clear canopy. When the room suddenly became bathed in iridescent light, Rick spun around to investigate the source.

He was startled to see the little boy standing before him grinning from ear to ear with his hands behind his back. Rick smiled, in spite of himself, as he tried to regain his composure.

"Hey, little man!" he said, taking a small step closer. "We've been looking for you. You shouldn't be down here all by yourself."

He looked at the spaceship and then back to the little boy before he continued, "It isn't safe. Are you alone?"

The boy simply nodded yes.

'Okay, then. You should come with me back upstairs. No one is going to hurt you. We just want to talk and maybe get you something to eat. Are you hungry?"

Again, a simple nod yes from the boy.

"Well then, it's settled. We'll take care of you, I promise. Umm, what do you have there behind your back?"

The boy stopped grinning and brought his arms forward and lifted them up high to reveal that he was holding the heads of Cody and Bradley.

Horrified, Rick took a step backward while exclaiming, "Jesus! Oh, sweet Jesus! What the fuck have you done?"

He pulled his gun and said, "What the fuck are you?"

The little boy casually tossed the heads aside and revealed his true form. Rick screamed and began firing at the creature. He did not stop until his weapon was empty.

At that same moment, Donald and Stephen had made their way into the basement and once they heard the shots, ran towards Rick's location to investigate.

Upon arrival, they saw the monster dragging Rick by the feet towards its spaceship. Rick spotted them and screamed, "Help me! Help me please! It killed Cody and Bradley!"

That's when Stephen spotted his comrades' heads on the ground and yelled, "Oh, dear GOD!"

By the time Donald pulled his gun and aimed to shoot, the creature had entered his ship with a still screaming Rick and the ship came to life, clearly ready to take off.

"Come on, Stephen!" Donald said. "We have to get out of here and we have to get out of here now!"

"But…" Stephen was clearly flabbergasted at everything he had just witnessed.

"There's not a damn thing that we can do for them now! Let's go!"

Stephen said, "Okay," and the pair ran as quickly as they could back upstairs and upon reaching the ground floor, could feel the whole building vibrating. They barely made it back outside into the snow and cold air when the warehouse simply imploded.

The creature's spaceship broke through the rubble and shot up into the night sky. In a flash of light, it was gone in an instant.

Less than forty-eight hours later, Donald and Stephen were sipping drinks on a beach in Cancun, Mexico. Neither of them had spoken about the events that transpired back in Philadelphia since the incident. They thought they were going to put the experience behind them and get on with their lives, but as night began to fall, locals and tourists alike were becoming hysterical.

Perplexed, they asked someone what the matter was. All the individual did was point to the sky. The pair looked up and were immediately hit with a sense of dread. There appeared to be hundreds of ships entering the atmosphere. Identical to the ship that left that abandoned warehouse in Philadelphia in ruins.